DEADLY HOLIDAY

Strong Women, Extraordinary Situations
Book Three

Margaret Daley

Deadly Holiday
Copyright © 2014 Margaret Daley

http://www.margaretdaley.com/

ONE

Tory Caldwell released a long breath. *Ah, a weekend to do nothing but relax and rest. The best gift I could have right now after the past four months. If only that were possible...*

After dropping her ten-year-old son Morgan off to spend the weekend with his best friend, Tory headed down the mountain toward Crystal Creek, a little town nestled at the bottom of a mountain in the Colorado Rockies. Although mid-December, the next few days were supposed to be above freezing with no chance of snow, so Morgan had pleaded with her to let him stay with Josh, who lived at nine thousand feet.

As she navigated the curvy two-lane road, she mentally ticked off her long list of chores and Christmas shopping to be completed before she returned to school on Monday.

Four-thirty Friday afternoon, and it was already starting to get dark. She didn't like to drive this highway at night. Glancing out her rearview mirror, she glimpsed a black sports car speeding around the curve and coming right toward her, at least fifteen miles over the speed limit. When it was practically on her bumper, she noticed the driver's irritated face. All of a sudden, the young, blond headed man, no more than twenty, gunned his vehicle and passed her at the start of the most twisty part of the highway.

Tory gasped, gripping the steering wheel.

The reckless driver zipped in front of her, nearly clipping her bumper. She'd barely registered the car's license plate—HOTSHOT—when it disappeared around the bottom of the S-curve. She breathed easier, knowing at least she didn't have to worry about him riding her tail.

When she hit a straight stretch of the road, she spied the black sports car a hundred yards or so ahead. It was veering toward the drop-off on the right side of the highway. The driver swerved, over-compensated and bounded into the other lane—right toward an older gentleman walking on the shoulder next to the mountain.

The car hit the pedestrian. The man flew into the air.

"No!" Tory screamed.

The older man struck the pavement, his body bouncing.

Stunned, Tory slammed on her brakes and skidded several feet while the driver of the sports car slowed for a few seconds, then revved his engine and sped away.

Tory guided her Jeep to the shoulder, parked, then climbed out, shaking so badly that she held her door until she was steady enough to move. A chilly wind cut through her as she crossed to the man lying face up in a pool of blood. He stared up at her with lifeless eyes.

She knelt, and with a trembling hand, she felt for a pulse at the side of his neck. Nothing. She tried again. Still no pulse. Then she hovered her fingertips over his slightly open mouth. No breath. She wished she knew CPR, but from the looks of him she didn't think it would have mattered.

She straightened and scanned the area. Deserted. Except for the black sports car, she hadn't seen any other vehicles since she'd started back to Crystal Creek. Not a lot of people lived on the top of this side of the mountain.

As she took one final sweep of her surroundings, she spied a wallet and set of keys not far from the older gentleman. She picked up the brown billfold and flipped it open to see if there was any identification. A photo of a man who looked like the one on the pavement declared the victim was Charles Nelson, seventy-two years old. The address indicated he lived nearby. He had probably been on his way home. Since this was a crime scene, she returned the wallet to where she found it. She shouldn't have touched it in the first place, but at least she could tell the 911 operator who the victim was.

Shivering, she dug into her coat pocket and removed her phone, praying she had driven far enough toward the main highway to get cell reception. No bars. Dead as the man at her feet.

She could return to Josh's house, but she knew a gas station/grocery store was closer down the mountain. If there wasn't cell reception, the place would have a landline phone she could use. Not wanting to involve her son in this, she chose to continue toward the highway.

Ten minutes later, she sat in the store's parking lot and punched in 911 on her cell phone. After she reported the hit-and-run, she took a few minutes to compose herself. Her hands were still shaking. She'd never seen a wreck like that. She went inside to use the restroom and grab something hot to drink. Then she headed back up the mountain to wait for the police. When she arrived at the spot of the hit-and-run thirty minutes later, all she found was the blood on the pavement. The body was gone.

* * *

Tory used the police officer's large body to block the biting edge of the wind sweeping down the road, the lights on his patrol car the only illumination in the dark that settled on the mountain. "Sergeant Bennett, I know what I saw. A man named Charles Nelson lay dead right there." She pointed to the bloody spot.

The police officer took his flashlight and shone it on the spot. "Then where is this dead man? Did he get up and walk away?"

"If he's dead, obviously not." On the side closest to the drop off, she stared down into the valley, dark except for a few scattered lights. Could she have been wrong about Mr. Nelson being dead? Could he have gotten up, been disoriented and fallen down the mountain? "I told you his address. If he did walk away," she tried to keep the sarcasm from her voice, but it leaked in, "I figure you need to check his house. Or," she gestured to the drop off, "check down this ravine. Mr. Nelson was hit by a black sports car with a vanity license plate that read HOTSHOT. A young man with light blond hair drove away. Didn't even stop."

"There isn't a crime without a body. Did you start celebrating the weekend a little early?"

"If you're referring to drinking, I don't drink alcohol, so no. I'm not the criminal here. I'd find the person driving the sports car."

"And charge him with what? There is no body. That blood could be from an animal."

"Test it. It's not." Anger welled to the surface. She'd never been doubted like this before. Maybe it hadn't been a good idea to move to Crystal Creek last August. The town was beautiful and quaint, but the people weren't too inviting to newcomers.

Sergeant Bennett frowned, a skeptical expression in his eyes. "Officer Ward is on his way. We'll check it out, but there are some things that will have to wait until daylight. I have your information, if I find a body and need to contact you later. You're free to go."

"Just like that. I witnessed a hit-and-run."

"Do you want me to take you to the station?"

"No, but I know what I saw. Please check out the sports car driver. He may have been drinking. He weaved all over the road and sped dangerously fast."

"Lady, I know how to do my job."

Biting the inside of her cheek to keep from retorting her doubts, she started for her car. That whole conversation didn't feel right. What was up with Sergeant Bennett? She glanced back and added, "I'd like to be informed of your progress. Please."

"Sure. I don't have anything better to do than stop by every evening and give you an update to a hit-and-run that doesn't have a body." His sarcasm dripped off every word.

It would do no good to give a snappy comeback. *Let it go, Tory*. She continued to her Jeep as another patrol car appeared. Maybe Officer Ward would do a better job.

* * *

Tory took her anger out on the house as she nailed in the clips to hold her Christmas lights around her door and porch, the extent of her outdoor decorations. Even Jordan Steele, her neighbor, had outlined his whole house yesterday in white lights and laid some in his front bushes. She'd never figured he'd participate in the challenge to have all the houses in the subdivision decked out for the holidays, but last night his quite tasteful display of simplicity dared her to put something up, even if it was only two or three strings of red lights.

Two years ago, even though her husband had been fighting cancer, he'd been outside putting up the Christmas decorations because Morgan loved the wonderland he created in their front yard. She'd never forget finding him on the ground. He'd collapsed. She'd rushed him to the hospital. He'd died a month later.

Her pounding echoed through the air, but she gave the last plastic clip an extra hit. She imagined the bald headed Sergeant Bennett's face with his dark bushy eyebrows as she hit the nail. "Why don't..." pound, pound "...you believe me?"

"I don't think your house is going to answer back." The deep masculine voice startled her.

She jerked around and almost lost her balance on the stepladder. Flapping her arms, she regained her steadiness, but not before Jordan Steele moved forward and put his hands around her waist. There'd always been a polite casualness between them when they'd talked out in the yard, but he'd never gotten that close. His touch was even more startling than his voice had been a moment earlier.

"Who doesn't believe you?"

Cheeks flaming, Tory descended the short ladder and sat on its top step. "The police, or rather, Sergeant Bennett. He told me today when I called that I must have imagined the hit-and-run I witnessed yesterday."

"Where?"

"The north face of the mountain. I was

returning from taking Morgan to stay the weekend with his friend." She pointed to the rocky structure dominating Crystal Creek's landscape. "A young man ran Charles Nelson down on the road. The driver killed Mr. Nelson but kept going, barely slowing down. I saw the whole thing."

Surprise flittered across Jordan's expression. "And this sergeant didn't believe that was what happened? How did he explain the dead body?"

Twisting her mouth in an exasperating look, Tory averted her gaze. "There was a small problem. I had to go farther down the mountain to get cell reception to call 911. When I returned to the scene of the hit-and-run, Mr. Nelson's body was gone, along with his keys and his wallet, which had flown out of his coat pocket." The police might not believe her, but the Lord knew she was telling the truth, and somehow she would convince the rest of the world too.

"There wasn't a trace of the man? Maybe he wasn't dead and somehow got up."

Tory shook her head. "Impossible. I've had first aid training. I know how to check for a pulse. Besides, there was blood on the pavement, which was still there when I came back half an hour later."

"What did the police officer say about the blood?"

"He thinks it's from a deer or something."

"Is he going to test it?"

"I insisted he test to see if it's human. He said he would, but I think he just said that to humor this crazy lady." Tory patted her chest. "I called Sergeant Bennett when I didn't hear anything this morning. He told me Mr. Nelson lives with his son and daughter-in-law, and they said that the man went to see his brother until after the holidays. Every year the two brothers go hunting north during this time. The couple's place is up the road from where the hit-and-run occurred. The police sergeant wasn't happy I still insisted there was a hit-and-run. On the phone I could hear him muttering a few unkind words under his breath."

A dark glint flared in Jordan's deep brown eyes. "Some people don't like to have their authority challenged."

"I'm not letting this go. A person ran down that man and killed him. The driver was reckless—he didn't even get out of his car to see if Mr. Nelson was alive. I'm going to stop at the Nelsons' house and do my own questioning. I know what I saw. I dreamed about it last night." She shuddered at the memory of the nightmare that had awakened her early this morning.

"You shouldn't go alone. What if something else is going on?"

"What are you doing tomorrow afternoon? Care to take a trip up the mountain?" The invitation came out without her thinking it through. Her neighbor usually kept to himself. Sure, they'd had a few casual conversations in the yard, often about his rental property, the house she lived in.

"If you insist on going, I'll go with you."

Elated she would have a witness when she confronted the Nelsons, she smiled, pushing down the urge to hug him for his assistance. "Thanks."

"No problem." One corner of his mouth tilted up. "I came over here to help you with your lights. I wouldn't want you falling off the ladder on my rental property."

Tory's grin widened. The day was looking up after a rocky start. "I accept your offer. I may be crazy, but I'm not stupid."

* * *

Sunday afternoon, Jordan set his empty coffee mug on the coaster on the end table then stretched on the couch. He'd been sitting most of the morning. Dutch, his German shepherd, came up and dropped a red ball in his lap.

"Sorry, boy, I promised my tenant I'd go with her today. She fancies herself a private detective or something."

Thinking about Tory Caldwell brought a smile to his lips. She was a plain Jane, but there was a spirit about her that intrigued him—or would, if he were interested in a woman. He wasn't. He had his hands full trying to keep his life together. With Dutch, his service dog, he'd made strides toward healing from the post-traumatic stress disorder that came home with him from Afghanistan two years ago. Most of his squad hadn't come back to the States. He was the lucky one—or so people kept telling him. He didn't feel that way. His battle buddies had died when a bomb landed on the building they were in. Their screams still rang in his mind when it quieted enough to let the sounds in.

When he heard a sharp knock on his front door, he shook off those memories. He tried not to dwell on what had happened in the war zone, but sometimes the flashbacks would come out of nowhere. He rubbed Dutch on the top of his head, feeling the calming connection with his dog, then rose to let his tenant into his house.

Tory's smile and sparkling green eyes greeted him when he pulled the door open. The sight lifted his spirits just as their occasional talks over the past few months had. He stepped to the side to allow her inside. Her gaze stopped at his dog.

"This is Dutch. You've probably seen him around. He looks ferocious, but he's a cuddly teddy bear."

"Thank goodness you put Teddy in front of bear, because I've encountered a few hiking, and have kept my distance." Tory held her hand out for his dog to sniff, then scratched him behind his ear and gained a new best friend.

"He likes you."

"Good thing, because I wouldn't want a German shepherd mad at me. Ready? I'm supposed to pick Morgan up in an hour, but I'd like to stop and talk with the Nelsons beforehand. I haven't said anything to my son about seeing that hit-and-run. It didn't seem like something to talk about over the phone."

"True. Maybe we can get to the bottom of it today."

Tory turned to leave, zipping up her blue parka, her long blond hair peeking out from under her white beanie. "A cold front is moving in."

"The weather report calls for snow in

the middle of the week."

"That'll just make my dazzling display of fifty lights a must-see on all the Christmas light tours."

"I looked at it last night, and I thought it was nice."

She laughed. "Your outside decorations are nice. Mine are adequate and will keep Mr. Foster from bugging me for not participating in the neighborhood light challenge. I was the last holdout. When you caved in, I thought I should too."

"I'm with you. It's easier to comply than deal with Mr. Foster's little notes in your mailbox."

"It's sad he thinks these decorations are what Christmas is really about."

"I'm not sure what he believes. All I know is that he wants this to be the best neighborhood in Crystal Creek."

She groaned. "Then I didn't do enough. Why didn't you warn me before I moved in to this neighborhood?"

He tried an apologetic grin. "Sorry."

Jordan locked up and followed Tory to her Jeep in the open garage. Usually he took Dutch with him everywhere, but she was driving and had just met his service dog, and she didn't even know it was a service dog. That was a conversation he didn't start with people. He filed it under *none of their business*.

As he slipped into the front passenger's seat, he said, "Send Mr. Foster to me if he says anything about your display. I'll sic Dutch on him."

"I thought your dog was a cuddly Teddy bear."

"Usually, but he's also protective and well-trained."

"Good to know. Morgan has been bugging me about getting a dog." She backed out of her driveway and headed toward the highway. "We had one where we lived previously, but he died right before we moved."

"What kind?"

"A Yorkie, always in everyone's business. What made you get a German shepherd?"

Jordan deepened his voice. "He's a manly dog for a manly man. None of them little yippy critters for me." He winked at her, so she'd know he was joking. Admitting he had PTSD had been tough enough, and even to looking into getting a service dog had made him feel weak that he couldn't get over it on his own. The first eight months back in the States, he'd tried to deny he had a problem. But when he'd stopped wanting to interact with people and ran his rental and investment business from home, only going out when absolutely necessary, the pastor from the church he grew up in came to visit him in Denver.

"Probably a good watch dog, too," Tory said.

"That's an added bonus." No need to mention that his pastor wouldn't give up on him until he sought help.

She slanted a look at him. "I imagine you know how to take care of yourself."

"If you're referring to my military training, then yes, I usually can." Usually being the key word. Nothing he could do for his comrades when those explosives bombarded them. The shrapnel scars on his left thigh and his terrible memories were all he had left from that day. More than most of the guys, who hadn't escaped at all.

He stared out the side window. He thanked God every day that his pastor had cared enough to keep coming back until he'd persuaded him to get help. Last December, he'd moved with Dutch to Crystal Creek for a fresh start.

When Tory started up the mountain, she glanced at him again. "Thank you for coming. I feel safe with you here."

Jordan tried to ignore the warmth those words made him feel.

"I'm not sure what to expect with the Nelsons," she continued. "I don't understand why they told the police Mr. Nelson was out-of-town. There must be an explanation or a misunderstanding."

"Or, for some reason, they're lying."

"Why would they lie? Unless the person in the sports car was related to them. The young man I saw was probably no more than twenty."

"I'm good with computers. I can look into the Nelson family if you don't get answers today."

"So you don't think I'm crazy?"

"Why would you lie about something like that? Before I rented that house to you, I checked your references." And more, but he wasn't going to tell her that. He had a lot of rental properties in Crystal Creek and the surrounding towns, and he did background checks all the time, but since she would be living next door, he went even further.

"What made you come over yesterday afternoon?"

"With all that pounding, I wanted to make sure you weren't tearing down my house."

She grinned. "You don't have that to fear from me. I don't have a lot of strength in my arms. Maybe I should take up weight lifting."

"Exercising is a great stress reliever." He should know. Hadn't he spent hours working out in the last couple of years? Just one more technique to keep him sane.

"And I intend to work it into my schedule—one day."

He glanced at her and smiled. "In the

distant future."

"Yep, you've got me pegged." As they climbed the mountain, Jordan noticed Tory stiffening, her grasp on the steering wheel so tight her knuckles were white.

This whole situation was strange. And intriguing. "I'd like to stop and look at the crime scene."

"Checking my story out?"

"No, but I've learned to get the lay of the land before going into battle."

"I suppose I do feel like that." She chuckled. "When I talked with the sergeant yesterday, he said the test results proved the blood on the pavement was from an animal. I'm going to try and get a sample of it. I know it wasn't an animal, and I intend to have my own lab test run on it."

"Oh, yeah? Do you know someone who can do that?"

"Not yet, but I'm sure I can find a lab somehow."

"I know a police detective in Denver who might be able to get it checked for you."

She slowed the Jeep and parked on the

shoulder of the two-lane road. As she climbed from the vehicle, she said, "Be careful stepping out. The drop off isn't too far away."

It had been a long time since anyone worried for his well-being. The gesture touched him and softened his war-weary heart. He climbed from the car, peeked past the guardrail, and whistled. "You weren't kidding. That'd be quite a fall."

As he rounded the rear of her Jeep, she kept her head lowered and swept her gaze over the pavement. Her brow wrinkled, and her mouth pinched together.

"It's gone. I know this is the right place. Mr. Nelson landed two feet from this rock formation." Pointing at the place, she looked toward him, her green eyes stormy. "Someone must have cleaned the blood up. Why?"

Had Tory really witnessed a hit-and-run? Or was she making it up? Or just crazy? But no—all the references he'd checked had given her glowing reports. Full of integrity. Caring. And nothing from their casual conversations had contradicted that.

He stepped nearer to her, wanting to erase the concern from her face. "Let's check for blood splatter on those rocks near the shoulder. If someone did clean up the road, he might not have thought about that."

While she went to the pile of stones, he knelt and examined the asphalt. In the service, he'd learned to track using all his senses. A slight odor of bleach teased his keen sense of smell.

"Nothing," Tory said with a sigh.

He rose and inspected the rock formation. Slightly to the right, a small evergreen bush grew. He scrutinized the foliage and found a couple of red drops. "This could be something." He took out his Swiss Army knife and cut off the branch. "Do you have a sack to put this in?"

"I have a bag from Christmas shopping yesterday."

Jordan accompanied Tory to the rear of her SUV. He carefully inserted the stem with a couple of leaves into the sack. "If a test confirms this is human blood, then it might help you to convince the police something is going on."

"Or they'll dismiss it because there's no way to tell when it got on the shrub."

"It rained last week, so that'll narrow the timeframe some. Over time, it would have dried and flaked off. This is pretty fresh. And if it's human, his DNA might be found on it. They'll have a hard time denying that."

"Right." Tory slid into the driver's seat and started the engine. "The address on Mr. Nelson's driver's license isn't far from here."

"Since you have the license plate of the sports car, why don't I check with my friend in Denver to see who owns the sports car?"

"You'd do that?"

"Sure. I'll call Gage this evening. No reason not to check the whereabouts of that car and the driver. I'm particularly interested in where they were Friday afternoon."

"Sergeant Bennett told me the owner had an airtight alibi. And get this—the sports car was reported stolen."

"When?"

"I don't know. He didn't share much with me."

"And he didn't tell you who owned it and what the alibi was?"

She shook her head and turned left down a gravel road leading to a large, once white house about five hundred yards from the highway. As she stopped in front of the rundown abode, a huge man with a full dark beard came out onto the slanting porch, pointed his rifle and glared.

TWO

Paralyzed behind the steering wheel, Tory turned wide eyes on Jordan. "This isn't a good sign."

"Maybe this isn't the right place."

"I saw *Nelson* painted on the mailbox. This has to be the place. What should we do?"

Instead of answering, Jordan opened the door and climbed out, his arms spread out to indicate he wasn't carrying a weapon. "We must be lost. Can you help us?"

The landowner chewed something for a moment, his sharp eyes assessing them, then spit out of the side of his mouth. "Who are ya looking for? We don't git too many visitors here."

"Charles Nelson. Do you know where he is?"

The man lowered his rifle. "Nope. He's been gone fer a while."

"When will he be home?"

The large man shrugged, but as Tory exited the car, the man's attention turned to her, his hands tightening on his weapon. "You best be goin'."

"But Charles Nelson does live here?" Her voice was squeaky on the last word, and she had to force herself not to look at the rifle.

"Who are ya?" The big man's stiff stance eased a little.

"Tory Caldwell."

"Why do ya want him?"

"It's a personal matter." A brisk wind coming off the mountain shivered down Tory's length.

"Personal with ya?" The landowner cackled. "No way. More likely a bill collector."

"No, I'm not." She stepped forward a

few paces. "Then he is here?"

"Dinna ya hear, Lady? I said he ain't here. Git off my property. Now." Tensing, the giant clutched the gun in front of his barrel chest, his stance threatening, the weapon aimed at her.

She threw a glance at Jordan, wanting answers but not sure how to get them.

He backed up toward the passenger door, his arms raised as though he were being arrested. "We're leaving."

Shaking, Tory followed, climbed in, and put the car in reverse. As soon as the doors both closed, she backed away.

When she turned around in the yard, Jordan said, "Floor it."

She glanced out the rearview mirror. The giant fixed his sight on her Jeep. Tory stomped on the accelerator, gravel spewing everywhere.

A shot reverberated through the clearing. Scenes from her past flashed across her mind—David playing Frisbee with Morgan, David helping her make breakfast, her husband pulling her into his arms...

A shudder whipped down her. She waited for the impact of a bullet, a window to shatter. She pressed down on the pedal even more. The rear end fishtailed, but she didn't let up. When she turned onto the highway, she inhaled a decent breath and blew it out. Trembling set in.

"Hey, are you all right? Why don't I drive?"

She pulled over but didn't move from the driver's seat. "What happened back there?"

"We were shot at. I don't think he wanted us on his property."

"Who is he?"

"Good question and one I intend to find the answer to. I don't take kindly to being shot at."

A steel thread ran through Jordan's voice, but when she twisted toward him, she saw an ashen cast to his face. It probably mirrored her own expression. "I think we hit a touchy subject."

"I think you're right, which makes me wonder why." Jordan plowed his fingers through his short black hair. "Maybe he's hiding something."

She reached out and clasped his arm. "I'm sorry I dragged you into this. If anything had happened to you, I'd never forgive myself. You're only here because of me."

He glanced at her hand then into her eyes. "I'm glad you didn't come alone. Promise me you'll stay far away from that guy."

"I have a son who lost his father two years ago." The trembling increased as she considered what could have just happened to her, to Morgan. She swallowed hard, tears blurring her eyes. She swiped her hands across her cheeks. "I'm all he has, so I don't plan on doing anything stupid, especially after that."

"Good." One corner of his mouth tilted in a grin. "You're the kind of tenant a landowner wants, and I'd hate to lose you."

For just a second, she wanted to read more into that statement. Ridiculous. She barely knew Jordan. And no one could replace David.

She put the Jeep into drive and

continued to ascend the mountain. "I'm late picking up Morgan. I'm going to have to tell him about what I saw Friday. I grew up in a small town, and I know how fast news can make the rounds."

"So do you want me to dig into information about the Nelsons?"

"Yes, if you would. And call your friend in Denver about that car. Something's not right here. It looks like Charles Nelson didn't have much money, but he deserves a proper burial. No telling where his body is." She pulled into the driveway of Morgan's friend's house. "And I know what I saw. A man died on that road Friday afternoon."

"I'll do it if you promise me you won't do anything without letting me know. If something is wrong here, I don't want you putting yourself in danger. As you said, you have a son who depends on you."

Jordan's concern made her feel she wasn't so alone now without David. That first year after his death had been the most difficult time of her life. She wouldn't have gotten through it without the Lord. The way she'd found her teaching job at Crystal

Creek Elementary, stumbling into the perfect house to rent—those had God's hand all over them. And for the past four months, she and Morgan had been doing a lot better. Until Friday.

"I promise. I only want to ask some questions. Maybe the Nelsons found the body and got rid of it for some reason. They didn't commit the crime. Believe me. That sports car was expensive. Not something they could afford from the looks of their property."

"If I can't come up with anything concrete, will you let it go?"

What else could she do? "Yes."

Morgan came out of the house and hurried toward the Jeep. When he saw Jordan sitting in the front seat, he climbed into the back. "Hi, Jordan. I didn't expect to see you here with Mom."

"I figure we might have some time to get in a basketball game before it gets dark. I didn't get a chance to run today, and I need some exercise."

"You two play basketball together?" Tory headed for the road.

"Yep. I told you, Mom, that me and Josh played with Jordan and some other guys on the court down the street. Jordan is really good. He's been giving me some pointers."

"Oh, that's right. I remember you saying something a couple of weeks ago." She must be more rattled than she realized.

"Where's Dutch?" her son asked.

Jordan glanced back at Morgan. "He's at home."

"When are you going to start working on your Mustang?"

"This week. You can help if you want."

"Really! Mom, can I?"

"If Jordan says it's okay, then it's fine with me. I know how much you love cars." Tory tensed as she neared the spot where the hit-and-run had occurred.

"What male doesn't," Jordan said with a laugh.

"She's a girl. To Mom a car is for taking you places. That's all."

They passed the spot, and Tory forced lightness into her voice. "What do you *boys* think a car is?"

"The right car is a work of art. Its sleek lines, the way it moves." Jordan angled toward Morgan. "Right?"

"Yeah. A Mustang is a classic."

Tory chuckled. "You two are hopeless."

As Jordan and Morgan discussed restoring the '65 Mustang in his garage, she realized her son had adjusted to life in Crystal Creek better than she had in the four months they'd lived there. With the move, then teaching a different grade at a new school, she'd been so focused on her work, she'd let other things slip.

Christmas was a good time to reach out to others, starting with Jordan. Anyone who was willing to help her with the hit-and-run and reach out to her son was worth knowing.

* * *

At school Monday, Tory sat at her desk and ate her lunch while she worked on a few special activities for the last week before Christmas break. Her third graders were counting down until Friday. She was no better, though. She was counting the minutes until school was out, because she'd invited Jordan over for dinner. She put her Christmas activities aside and started on a grocery list for tonight.

Morgan was excited Jordan had agreed to come. Her son needed a male role model. He and David had spent so much time together, playing basketball and wrestling in the yard. Watching Morgan's hope whither while David's cancer rapidly got worse had broken her heart. Morgan took his father's death harder than she had. Until she'd seen her son and Jordan playing basketball at the park yesterday, she hadn't realized how much Morgan needed a man in his life to do activities like that.

Her classroom door opened. Too early for the children to be returning to class from lunch and recess, Tory looked up and clenched her hands. Why was he here? On Saturday over the phone, Sergeant Bennett had implied again that she must be loco.

She stayed at her desk, making him

come to her across the room. "Have you discovered something new? Like Charles Nelson's body?"

The police officer frowned, his bushy eyebrows slashing almost together. "What body?"

"The one you can't find. Did you call Charles Nelson's brother to see if he was there like his son said?"

The sergeant's eyes narrowed. "Sarcasm doesn't become you. Like the man's son said, no one answered because they're on their yearly hunting trip, which I've seen pictures of on the wall at the Nelsons' place. I've left several messages to call me as soon as possible. Nothing so far."

She felt as if she lived in a parallel universe where all the laws of nature were different. None of this made sense. "Thank you for letting me know. Now if you'll excuse me, I have work to do before the children return."

"I have one more piece of business." He withdrew a folded piece of paper from his back pocket and laid it on the desk near her.

"What's that?"

"A restraining order."

THREE

Tory held her emotions inside while she finished teaching for the day, but her blood boiled at the gall of the Nelson family. Charles's son, Bart, was the one who'd shot at her and Jordan. If anyone had a right to get a restraining order against someone, it was she.

Her hands hurt from gripping the steering wheel so tightly as she drove to the grocery store and then home. She'd wanted to vent to the police sergeant, but her class came back early. Maybe that short rain at noon had kept her from saying something she would have regretted.

Exhausted, Tory drove into her

driveway, spying Jordan working on his car next door. He wore a black T-shirt and jeans, his muscular biceps visible for her enjoyment, although the December temperature was in the forties. Cold didn't seem to bother him. Not like her—she was chilly on a sunny day in the low sixties.

He looked toward her and smiled. Her pulse accelerated as she waved and pulled into the garage. Jordan wasn't classically handsome. He was rugged with an air of self-assurance. Being an ex-Navy SEAL, he no doubt could take care of any situation thrown his way, whereas her idea of exercise was making it through a day as a third grade teacher. What would he say about the restraining order? Had he gotten one, too?

As she climbed from her Jeep, he stepped into her garage and asked, "Something wrong?"

"How can you tell?"

"Your scowl and those lines between your eyebrows."

She peered at herself in the side mirror. With a deep, composing breath, she relaxed her facial muscles. "Is this better?" She opened the back of the Jeep to retrieve the groceries.

"Much better." He grabbed two sacks from the rear of her car.

"Did you get a restraining order today?"

"No. Did you?" He walked with her toward the door into the house.

"From the Nelson family. I obviously terrified them with my menacing presence yesterday."

"They moved fast. It's only been twenty-four hours since we were there, and if anyone was menacing, it was me." He stopped in the middle of the kitchen and faced her. "I don't think you know how to look menacing."

"I might before this is over, but thank you for saying that. I needed to hear something good today. Even I'm beginning to doubt my sanity. Sergeant Bennett told me he tried Charles's brother a couple of times, but there was no answer, as though that verified what Bart Nelson had said about the hunting trip." The headache that had started when she saw the sergeant in

41

her classroom had grown and now was pounding against her skull.

Jordan put the sacks on the counter and began emptying them. "There's something fishy going on. I went to Denver and gave Gage the foliage we found. He'll let me know something as soon as he gets the results. When I got back, I spent a couple hours on my computer digging up information."

"What did you discover?"

"Gage told me who the car was registered to with the license tag HOTSHOT, and I came home to do some research on him."

"Really? Who?"

"Peter London."

"Any connection to Harold London?"

"His eldest son. He's in his second year at Colorado State."

Tory whistled. "Harold London owns more than half this town. That fact puts a whole new spin on all of this."

"It could, and we need to keep that in mind as we move forward."

"We?"

He leaned against her counter and crossed his arms. "I was in that Jeep when Bart Nelson shot at us. I'm in this, too."

"Could Harold London have paid the Nelson family to cover up their father's death?"

"It's possible. Money makes people forget a lot of things, even family members." Jordan carried some items that needed to be kept cold to the counter by the refrigerator. "I discovered that Peter has been arrested twice for DUI. One of those times he wrecked his car, hitting a parked vehicle and a garage."

Tory massaged her temples. "Was anyone hurt?" The whole situation was becoming complicated.

"When Peter left the party, there was a passenger, Nathan, in the car. Peter and this guy were housemates. The police didn't indicate anyone on the traffic report, though, but Nathan left college the next day in the middle of the semester. I wonder if Peter's buddy had been injured, and the London family whisked him out of town then paid him off."

"It's serious when you have one DUI, let alone three if you count Friday's accident."

"With his record of drinking and driving, Peter would have been in serious trouble with vehicular homicide added to a DUI charge."

"And I was the only witness."

"Looks like it. But it still doesn't make sense. Where's the black sports car? If it hit someone, there'll be evidence on it, not to mention some damage. We need to find it. I'll ask my friend to put a BOLO out on it. Gage has some connections with the state police."

"He won't get in trouble?"

"He knows how to work the system. Believe me, this guy hates seeing anyone get away with a crime."

"How do you know him?"

"We grew up together. Even as a child he wanted to be a police officer."

"I feel like Gage. I don't want to see the driver get away with Charles Nelson's death." Tory stuck the last of the groceries away then sank against the counter, closing her eyes. It didn't help the thumping against her skull.

"What's wrong?"

"The stress of the past few days is catching up in one killer headache, and my medication doesn't seem to be touching it."

"Sit at the table and let me see if I can help. I know a thing or two about stress headaches."

She pulled out a chair and eased down.

"Relax," he said.

"Easy for you to say."

"I know it's hard with all that's happened, but try."

With more deep breaths, she managed to ease the tension in her shoulders. Then Jordan's large hands began to rub the back of her neck, head and shoulders. She wanted to melt. He knew how to give a good massage, but his warm touch affected her beyond that.

As he worked his fingers into her taut muscles, he said, "Is it helping?"

"Definitely. Be careful. I might be knocking on your door every day for this." She sighed. "What I want to know is what kind of airtight alibi Peter London would have had? It's easy to say the car was stolen."

"You're not very good at relaxing, are you?"

She tried to ease her stiff shoulders. "I think it's time we ask the young man where he was on Friday and when he reported his car stolen."

The stress began to flow from her, and for a moment, she lost her train of thought, suddenly focusing a lot of energy on the man standing behind her. She forced her mind back to the problem. "I don't think Peter intentionally killed Charles Nelson, but with his prior DUIs, he needs to be taken off the road. He needs to get help. He obviously has a drinking problem, and it's dangerous to others. So how do we prove what I saw?"

Jordan stopped and sat in the chair catty-cornered from Tory, concern darkening his brown eyes. "Let me see what I can discover about the car and what we hear from Gage. I don't want you doing anything until we have some hard evidence. You're probably right about Peter London. The guy might be guilty of killing someone and covering it up, but he's not somebody you want to mess with."

"I'd understand if you don't want to get involved anymore."

"I'm already involved. When I start something, I finish it. Give me some time. No investigating without me. Okay?"

As she stared into his eyes, his look drew her in, as if he'd wrapped his arms around her and held her close, keeping her safe. "You'll let me know what you find?"

"Yes."

The front door banged open. "Mom, I'm home." Morgan called out.

"I'm in the kitchen." She turned to Jordan. "He has basketball practice right after school on Monday and Wednesday, and Josh's mother drops him off."

Morgan stepped into the room, shed his coat, and hung it up on a peg near the door to the garage. "I'm starving. When is dinner?"

Tory laughed, pushing away the stress from the sergeant's visit to school. "In an hour. I have to make it first, and it's only five o'clock."

Her son went to the refrigerator and withdrew the orange juice. "Jordan, we have an hour to kill. Want to play some basketball?"

"You aren't sick of it after practice?" Tory rose, part of her missing the bond with Jordan she'd experienced a minute ago. But her cautious side realized it was probably a good thing her son had come home when he did. She'd just begun to put her life together, and now with witnessing the hit-and-run, she had more than enough problems to deal with.

"Never, Mom. I want to play basketball professionally. I've got to practice a lot."

Jordan stood. "I'm up for some basketball."

Her son grinned from ear to ear and headed out of the kitchen. "We'll be back right before dinner."

After Morgan left with Jordan, Tory began fixing spaghetti, trying to put the hit-and-run from her mind for the time being. But she couldn't dismiss what she and Jordan had discussed earlier. Something was wrong, and she intended to find out what. If the police wouldn't look further into it, she would. She saw the man get hit. That was not a hallucination.

* * *

The sun disappeared behind the mountains to the west of Crystal Creek. The view from the top was spectacular but with dusk setting in, Tory could barely see the lake south of town.

"I'm glad your neighbor could watch Morgan on such short notice." Jordan passed through the iron gates onto the London's property.

"I can't believe you called Harold London this morning and set up a meeting so fast."

"Well, you seemed adamant yesterday, and I'm just as curious as you are."

"That's because Sergeant Bennett thinks I'm seeing things, and it certainly didn't help that the blood test came back saying it was an animal. If I didn't know what I saw, I'd say I was crazy too."

"Let's hope the test on the foliage comes back human blood."

"If it comes back as animal blood, I don't know what I'm going to do."

As they neared the London mansion, Tory closed her eyes and thought about her tranquil place that always calmed her when her nerves were stretched to the snapping point. In her mind she saw Christ in a mountain meadow with thousands of wildflowers blooming. He stood with his arms wide, welcoming her into his embrace, giving her the comfort she needed—the serenity she sought.

"Don't worry about that until it happens." Jordan parked his SUV in front of the house. "I didn't mention to Harold London that I was bringing you. I don't know if he knows about our friendship or not."

"And he agreed to see you out of the blue like this?"

"He's wanted to meet with me for months, so when I called, he saw his opportunity. I have a piece of land he wants to buy."

"I wonder if he knows what I look like."

"I bet he does. You've implicated his son's car in a hit-and-run."

"When I dropped off Morgan, good thing I told Mrs. Scott where we were going, in case something happens."

Jordan lifted his hand and cupped the side of her face, his eyes warm as they took in her features. "London is a renowned Colorado businessman. I doubt he would be that blatant."

Tory smiled, the feel of his fingers against her cheek tempting her to forget why they were sitting in front of Harold London's mansion. "Okay, that may have been a bit melodramatic, but this time last week, I would never have dreamed what was going to happen. This has all been surreal."

"Let's hope we get some answers. Ready?" His hand slipped away, and he opened his door.

For a few wild seconds, she thought of grabbing him and keeping him in the car, but she needed those answers, especially after today at school. Her principal, Mr. Mayne, had stopped by her class twice unexpectedly, as though he were keeping an eye on her. What else could have prompted that? Someone must have called him about her.

She climbed from the SUV and walked with Jordan to the massive front doors, carved with an intricate wildlife scene.

The man who let them into the house didn't look like a butler but a bodyguard. Big and muscular with a gun in a holster at his waist. She gulped at the sight of the weapon.

They were left alone in a formal living room—elegant, richly–appointed, and cold. She made a full circle, taking in all the artwork hanging on the walls. She paused at one photograph of a couple and Peter. She'd looked at a picture on the Internet of Peter London. This photo confirmed the similarities, except for the hair color, between whom she saw driving the car and Peter. She knew hair color could be changed, but the picture on his Facebook page had been taken the week before and his hair had been dark brown then. Was she wrong about Peter?

"I think he knows I was coming. Most people in a business situation wouldn't welcome a person with a gun."

"The camera at the front gate would have shown him who was in the car. If he hadn't known before then, he does now. And I understand the man has two bodyguards with him at all times."

"Is that normal for businessmen?"

"It can be."

"That's sad."

"Why do you think that?"

"To live like that, in fear all the time that someone will come after you." Tory glimpsed Harold London in the entrance.

"But as you see, Mrs. Caldwell, I don't have the bodyguards with me now, so that must tell you I'm not afraid of you."

The underlying threat hung in the air between them. Tory straightened, squaring her shoulders. "That's good to know, considering you have no reason to be afraid of me."

Harold smiled, but it was strained and

cold. He turned to Jordan and shook his hand. "I was informed you brought a companion to our meeting, so I'm guessing this isn't going to be a discussion about that piece of land."

"No, but I would like to set up another time to talk to you about it, if you're still interested."

"I am. Have a seat." Harold sat and gestured toward the chairs across from him. "So why are you here?"

Before Jordan could say anything, Tory said, "I understand your son owns a black sports car with HOTSHOT tags. I witnessed a hit-and-run with that car last Friday. When was the car stolen?"

Harold's dark eyes glinted with a hard edge. "I've already talked with the police. I don't owe you an explanation."

"I realize that, Mr. London, but an old man was killed, and I want some answers for his family. If it happened around the time that I saw the man get hit, I might be a witness to help you find who stole the car."

"Until Sergeant Bennett showed up at

my house Friday night, I didn't even realize it had been stolen, but when I went to show the police officer the car, it wasn't there. My son had been inside all evening. He's home for Christmas break. My wife and I saw him several times that afternoon, and two of my employees did, too. So if you're thinking he was involved, he wasn't." The tall, distinguished man rose and turned his attention to Jordan. "If you *alone* decide to have a meeting about your property, make an appointment with my secretary. Now if you'll excuse me, we have a family commitment tonight, and I need to get ready. Bruce will show you two out."

As Harold left, the man who opened the front door earlier came to the entrance. Silent and menacing.

While they were escorted from the house, Jordan scanned the living room and the foyer. Bruce stayed on the deck, watching as they climbed into Jordan's SUV. When they passed through the gates, another large man stood at the side of the gate, a rifle cradled in his arms—much like Bart Nelson's had on Sunday.

Tory shuddered. "Since there's a chance someone stole the car and ran Charles Nelson down, I thought I worded the question as if that was what we were thinking."

"I can't imagine that car being stolen. This place is a fortress. If someone wanted to steal the sports car, why did they wait until he came home, when I'm sure it would have been easier to take it while he was at college? I know he has an expensive car, but there are easier targets out there than Peter's."

"Maybe this wasn't a good idea." Did she have the wrong guy?

"We learned a couple of things tonight. First, Sergeant Bennett believed you enough to come and ask Harold London about the car. Plus, we discovered the approximate time the car was stolen as well as the alibi. I'll check around and see when Peter left school for the holidays."

"Could one of the employees have been driving?"

He shrugged. "I suppose. But you saw a young guy in the car."

"I'm not sure it was Peter. Last night after you left, I looked on the Internet for a photograph of him and found one. The driver looked similar, but the hair isn't right. What if I'm wrong?"

"Don't start doubting yourself. Harold has learned to intimidate people with a look or his tone of voice. I'm going to talk with Gage and see what's going on about finding the sports car. There could still be evidence of the hit-and-run on it."

"I guess first we have to prove there was a hit-and-run before the authorities will investigate. And the only reason the good sergeant probably looked into Friday night was because he didn't have the test back on the blood on the road."

Jordan stopped at the light at the bottom of the mountain. "Let's get a pizza and try to forget the accident. What kind does Morgan like?"

She laughed. "The better question is, what kind doesn't he like? The answer is nothing."

"How about you?"

"Except for anchovies, I'm game for

anything, so order your favorite."

"Then everything except anchovies. Thin crust okay?"

"Sounds great."

Twenty minutes later when they arrived at Jordan's with an extra large supreme pizza, Tory crossed the street to get Morgan while Jordan set the table at his house.

When they were all seated, Tory blessed the food. She'd barely finished the *amen* before her son dug into the pizza.

"I'm starved. This is delicious." Morgan savored the next bite of his slice. "I thought you were gonna be gone longer."

"We got the information about the car right off." Tory poured a glass of milk for her son while she and Jordan drank water.

"Did it help you prove a man was killed?"

Her son knew she'd witnessed a wreck, but she hadn't gone into too much detail when she told him Sunday night. Every time she thought of Charles Nelson, she revisited the scene when she'd checked to see if he was alive—laying her fingers against his neck.

"A kid at school said you were seeing things. That there wasn't a wreck. I told him if you said there was one, then there was. He told me I didn't know what I was talking about. But I do, don't I?"

She set down her slice of pizza and leaned toward her son. "Yes, I saw a man on the side of the road hit by a reckless driver after I dropped you off."

"I knew it." Morgan popped the last bite into his mouth.

"How's basketball practice been going?" Jordan took several sips of his water.

Morgan answered and the two began talking about basketball and his latest game, effectively taking her son's mind off the hit-and-run. She shot Jordan a grateful smile and grabbed another slice of pizza.

Tory began to relax, and by the end of the meal, she'd managed to eat two slices and even contribute to the conversation about sports. When Morgan pushed back from the table, she said, "Did you finish your homework at Mrs. Scott's?"

"No, but I don't have much. Once I

complete it, can I watch TV afterwards?"

"One show, but I want to look at your homework before you put it up."

Morgan hopped to his feet and took his dishes to the counter before leaving the kitchen.

"He's a good kid."

"Yeah, I see a lot of David in him. They were close."

"What happened to your husband?"

Tory told him about David's intense battle with cancer. "We were best friends. Losing him knocked the wind out of me. I know what a good marriage is. My parents divorced when I was eleven, and I didn't see much of my father." She'd been determined when she'd married to work hard at her marriage, because all she could remember of her parents' was the arguing.

Jordan nodded sympathetically. "That must've been hard. My parents are happily married and retired. They live in the Bahamas."

"That must be a tough job. Right now, the beach sounds wonderful." She'd love to get away from what was going on in Crystal

Creek.

"I've been managing my father's properties in Colorado as well as my own. When I left the Navy, he retired." Jordan stood, grabbed both of their dishes, and carried them to the sink.

She stood and joined him at the counter. "What kind of properties?"

"Rentals, three resorts, office buildings, tracks of land, and two small shopping centers in Denver." Over half of what I manage is in Denver, but slowly I'm adding properties around this area."

"Why aren't you in Denver? That's a ninety-minute commute." Tory put their dishes in the dishwasher.

"There was a time I loved living in a big city, but now I relish the quiet and slower pace Crystal Creek offers. Besides, the drive to Denver is always beautiful. You can't beat the mountains."

"That's what drew me from Baltimore. I love the mountains. Not as fond of snow, but sometimes you have to take them together. This will be my first winter here."

"Do you have snow tires on your Jeep?

Provisions if you get stuck in a snowstorm?"

"Yes, to both questions. Remember? When I moved in, you gave me a list of what I should have in my car in case of an emergency."

"That's right. I forgot."

She hadn't forgotten. He'd taken the time to show her his provisions in the rear of his SUV. That was the first day she'd begun to see him more than her landlord. After that, they'd begun to talk more when they were outside. "I hope I never have an emergency to test whether or not I'm prepared, but I appreciated your guidance. I'd never lived on my own before David died. I went from college to being David's wife."

He finished wiping off the table, then hung up the washcloth on edge of the sink. His arm brushed against hers. The contact was brief but electric. She started to back away but stopped when he looked toward her. Less than a foot separated them. His gaze lured her closer. He shifted toward her.

He fingered her long blond hair behind her ears then framed her face. With his eyes smoldering like that, she felt roped to him, unable to move away even if she wanted to. And she didn't. She wanted him to kiss her.

Slowly he bent his head toward her and whispered his lips across hers. Tingles flashed down her. When he covered her mouth with his, she sank against him, her arms winding around him. As he deepened the kiss, she became lost in myriad of sensations—the faint smell of his lime scented aftershave, the roughness of his work-toughened hands, the taste of pizza on his tongue mingling with the coffee he'd had earlier.

"Mom, I'm finished," Morgan yelled from the direction of Jordan's den. "Come check it."

She pulled back, reluctantly dropping her arms to her sides. "He seems to feel right at home. Shouting is his personal intercom."

Jordan moved away from her, his chest rising and falling rapidly. "I'm glad he feels comfortable here."

"We'd better go home before I find him curled up on your couch asleep."

When she started for the hallway, Jordan's words stopped her in the doorway. "I'm not sorry I kissed you. You are an amazing woman."

She glanced over her shoulder with a smile. "I don't know about that, but I'm not sorry, either." As she made her way to Morgan, she hoped she'd schooled her features into a neutral expression, rather than one of a woman who had been thoroughly kissed by an intriguing man.

* * *

On Wednesday, Tory pulled into her driveway, tired and counting the days to Christmas break. Two more to go. She'd left school the instant the bell rang rather than staying her usual hour to work.

Her principal had paid her a visit to tell her there had been a complaint lodged against her by the parent of one of the children in her class. Mrs. Bates had said that she'd ridiculed her son in class the day before, but she hadn't. She'd asked him to be quiet once, but that was all. Then Mr. Mayne went on to tell her that he'd heard some alarming rumors about her. Apparently, he'd never had a teacher have a restraining order issued against her. Then, in his parting remark, he'd said that if all those rumors about her integrity didn't die down by the first of the year, more serious action would have to be taken against her. Their teachers were supposed to be above reproach.

She glanced toward Jordan's house, needing someone to talk to. His classic Mustang sat near the garage as though he'd been working on it, but he wasn't around. When had she come to depend on Jordan for his opinion? In five days, their relationship had evolved from acquaintances to friends and even more. She had a few co-workers she was getting to know, but in a short time, she realized Jordan topped the short list.

Maybe she needed to back off. Things were moving so fast. She hadn't fallen asleep last night for hours, her thoughts full of his kiss. Even today in class she'd daydreamed about it. She could call her sister or mother. Even though they lived across the country, they had always been there for her. She needed to stop depending on Jordan. She didn't want to become emotionally involved with anyone, not after her husband's death.

She snatched up her bag of papers that needed to be graded along with her purse and trudged toward the door into her kitchen. She would take a long, hot bath and try to relax before Morgan came home from basketball practice.

To help her wind down, lavender scented salts would be perfect in a bath. She'd make a calming cup of tea, too. Inside, after removing a gift from one of her third grade students, she set her tote on the table to go through later, then immediately filled a kettle with water and put it on the stove to boil.

She left it and made her way into the living room, where she placed the present under the Christmas tree, joining the other three gifts she'd already received from some of her students. At least it wasn't too barren. Her son's presents from her mother were beneath the branches, too. But this year would be a lean holiday. Moving across the country hadn't been cheap, and this job didn't pay what her previous one had. David's life insurance money was for Morgan someday, and she refused to dip into it. If she lost her job because of those nebulous rumors, what would she do?

The shrill whistle on the kettle startled her, and she gasped, her heart thudding against her ribs. Ever since she'd seen Charles Nelson run down, she'd felt jittery, especially with sudden sounds. And now with the knowledge of rumors about the restraining order flying around town, she had a reason to be concerned. The police not believing her was one thing, but now it was spreading to include her principal and staff at school. She hadn't told them about the restraining order, so who had?

She made her way toward the kitchen. If only she hadn't witnessed…But she had and would never forget the man who had stared up at her. Dead. She shook the image from her mind, the same one that had haunted her the last few nights.

After taking the water off the burner, she fixed her cup of tea, then headed for her bedroom with it. When she strolled into her room, she noticed the window was open a few inches. A chill flashed up her spine, and she backed a couple of steps toward the hallway. Suddenly her bedroom door rushed toward her as a burly man wearing a brown ski mask emerged from behind it.

Her gaze fastened onto his steely light blue eyes. Dead eyes. Fear froze her.

He held a knife in his right hand. The hall light gleamed off the blade.

Move. Now or never.

Urgency flooded her. She threw the hot tea in his face, then hurled the mug, too. She whirled around and raced for the front door.

Angry curse words blasted the air. The sound of pounding footsteps followed her, but she didn't dare look back. It would slow her down.

Escape, ten feet away.

Five.

Her hand grasped the knob, and she jerked the door open. The second her feet hit the porch, she shouted, "Help," again and again. She bounded down the porch steps.

Remembering Jordan had been working on his car earlier and might be back outside, she turned toward his house. She took two strides before her attacker tackled her, slamming her into the cold ground.

The air swooshed from her lungs at the hard impact.

FOUR

Tory tried to scream, but the sound died in her throat.

Her assailant's large bulk pinned her against the brown, prickly lawn, suffocating her with his weight. She couldn't draw any air into her lungs to call for help again. There was no way she could shove him off her. The trapped, helpless feeling sent panic racing through her body, fueling her resolve to get away. Morgan needed her. She twisted and clawed at her attacker, but he held her tight, his legs gluing her arms to her side.

A glove-clad hand gripped her neck and squeezed. The world tilted then spun before her eyes. *Help, Lord*.

Darkness lurked at the edges of her awareness. Her eyelids slid closed.

Suddenly the pressure on her chest lifted, and she heard flesh connecting with flesh through the haze of semi-consciousness. The noise penetrated her mind. Air rushed into her lungs, and her eyes bolted open.

Jordan and her attacker were locked in a bear hug until the man kicked out his leg and threw Jordan on the lawn, falling on him, the knife plunging toward his chest. He grabbed his assailant's arm, halting the weapon's downward trajectory.

When she scrambled to a crouch, lightheadedness assailed her, and she nearly collapsed back to the ground. She inhaled several deep gulps of oxygen-rich air, then focused on the two men wrestling. The knife in her assailant's hand quivered between the fighters.

She looked for anything to use against her attacker, but bark from her flowerbed wouldn't be an effective weapon. Then she remembered the cell phone in her pocket and pulled it out.

When the 911 operator came on, she reported the assault in progress on her lawn.

Jordan and her attacker rolled, and her neighbor ended up on top. Jaws clenched, Jordan squeezed the man's wrist tighter, forcing his arm with the knife out to the side. Then Jordan hammered their clasped hands into the ground. The weapon flew out of the assailant's grasp and landed a few feet from them. Jordan pounded his fist into the man's face, but he blocked the second jab and shoved Jordan off him.

They both pounced for the knife.

Jordan reached it first and gripped it.

Her attacker clambered to his feet and ran toward the street. Jordan raced after him, knife in hand.

The large man dove into a beat up black truck and started it. Jordan yanked on the door, but her assailant must have locked it. After the pickup peeled away from curb, the sound of sirens echoed in the late afternoon.

Jordan hurried to her. "Are you all

right?"

Tory hugged her arms across her chest, trying to stop shivering. She couldn't.

"Tory?"

She blinked, realizing he was waiting for her to say something. "I'll be okay. Just a few bruises." Her words came out as if another person were speaking for her. Tory was here, and yet part of her felt like an observer. Wishful thinking?

"What happened?" Jordan squatted next to her on the lawn.

The sound of the sirens grew nearer, and she thought back to that hit-and-run when she'd stood on the deserted highway at dusk waiting for the police to arrive. In fifteen minutes, not another car had come by. She'd hugged her arms that time too, staring at the dark shadows in the woods surrounding her as if someone were staring back at her. The reminder sent a shudder down her spine.

Jordan clasped her upper arms, drawing her full attention. "What happened?"

Focus on what Jordan's asking. I'm safe now. "I don't know. I came home from school and walked into my bedroom. He was behind the door and came after me with a knife."

"You were home earlier than usual. Maybe you surprised him. Maybe he was just a robber."

"Maybe. I don't know. It happened so fast. I didn't see anything out of place..." She closed her eyes and replayed what had happened. Stepping into her bedroom, seeing the man. Her hands trembled, and she clasped her knees against her chest. "The window was opened a few inches. I didn't do that. It should have been locked." She finally looked right at Jordan, his dark gaze like melted chocolate. It fixed on her with kindness. He had been here for her. "This definitely hasn't been my week." She tried to smile, but it didn't stay.

"I have to agree. Here let me help you up. The police are coming."

When he supported her as she stood, all she wanted to do was lean into him and forget the past fifteen minutes. Her body protested as though a steamroller had flattened her.

Two patrol cars parked in front of her house, and she recalled seeing both of those police officers at the scene of the hit-and-run. Moaning, she brushed the dirt and dead grass from her blouse and pants and waited while Sergeant Bennett approached her with Officer Ward, who was speaking on his handheld radio.

"Twice in a few days, Mrs. Caldwell. Trouble seems to follow you."

She stiffened at the condescending tone in the sergeant's voice. Anger rose to the surface, momentarily pushing all other emotions away. "A man was in my house. He attacked me when I fled. Thank heavens Jordan was home and saved me. At least this time I have a witness who can support what I said."

Sergeant Bennett assessed Jordan. "Are you the man who went with Mrs. Caldwell to the Nelsons' house on Sunday? You fit the description Mr. Nelson gave the police."

Jordan stiffened. "I just pulled a large man, probably weighing two hundred-thirty or forty pounds from Mrs. Caldwell. He was built like a linebacker and about six-feet-five. He wore a ski mask and has light blue eyes. He drove away in a black Ford truck with no license plate. And his breath smelled of garlic."

Amazed at Jordan's detailed description, Tory nodded her agreement. All she could remember were those blue eyes.

Officer Ward approached the sergeant, who turned to him. "I need you to check the premise for signs of forced entry and anything suspicious." He glanced at Tory. "I assume it's all right for him to go in and take a look around."

It wasn't a question, but Tory answered, "Yes. I think the guy came in through the window in my bedroom."

After the second man left, the sergeant zeroed in on Jordan. "You didn't answer my question."

"What does your question have to do with the fact that Mrs. Caldwell was attacked?"

Sergeant Bennett's eyes sharpened, and he stepped closer to Jordan. "It matters in another investigation. Is there a reason you're evading my question?"

A nerve jerked in Jordan's cheek. "I accompanied Mrs. Caldwell to see if Charles Nelson was all right, since she witnessed him being hit and thought he was dead. We were told he wasn't there, and we left. Nothing we did should have prompted Bart Nelson to shoot at the car as Mrs. Caldwell drove away. I was shocked that she received a restraining order. Something is very wrong with the way your department is handling this." Jordan drilled his look into the sergeant like a laser homing in on a cancerous spot.

"That's your story, not Bart Nelson's or his wife's."

Jordan held up the switchblade knife the intruder had carried. "My fingerprints will be on this, but possibly the assailant's, too. He brought this with him. I'd call that a solid lead for you to follow and figure out who he was."

The sergeant withdrew a latex glove and took the weapon.

Silence descended as the men measured each other.

Tory stepped between them. "What did

Bart Nelson say took place?"

"That you threatened his wife who you talked to first and wouldn't leave until he came out on the porch. Then you threatened him."

"You're kidding! First, we never saw his wife." Tory shook her head. "Why would I do that? What do I have to gain from all this?"

The sergeant opened his mouth then snapped it closed, looking up at the porch. "I didn't take the report, so I can't tell you any more than what I was told. But—"

Officer Ward stepped into the front doorway. "Sergeant, I need to show you something."

After securing the knife in an evidence bag, the bald-headed man walked toward her house, Tory followed with Jordan at her side. Maybe the intruder had taken something. Everything had happened so fast. She couldn't be sure of anything.

Entering her bedroom, Tory watched the younger officer lead the sergeant into the connecting bathroom. Had the intruder done something in there? Goose bumps shivered up her arms as she moved to the doorway to see what was going on. Right behind her, Jordan clasped her shoulder. It was all she could do not to lean into him.

"This is where you found that?" Sergeant Bennett asked the other cop as he put on a second latex glove.

"Yes. I haven't touched it. It was sitting out on the counter in plain sight. I haven't had a chance to look around. I started with the bedroom, because she said the window was open. They were both locked. After I looked around, I stepped in here and saw this."

The sergeant lifted the suspicious substance—a small zipper bag of white powder.

Tory gasped, speechless.

"Could be heroin or coke," Officer Ward said.

His words spurred Tory to protest. "That's not mine. The attacker must have left that. Maybe he was going to hide it, and I interrupted him before he could. Or it isn't drugs. I don't do drugs." Words tumbled from her as skepticism showed on the police officers' faces.

Sergeant Bennett confronted her with the packet in his hand. "I need you to go down to the station with me. I'll have the powder tested while you wait."

"Do you want me to search the rest of the house?" the young police officer asked.

"Wait outside until another officer arrives with a warrant. If this is a drug, I want to make sure we have everything covered."

"I haven't done anything wrong. Check for fingerprints on that bag. Mine aren't there. My son is coming home in half an hour." She was living a nightmare. Maybe she would wake up any moment, and everything would be back to normal.

When the sergeant pulled out his handcuffs, Jordan stepped into the bathroom doorway. "Is that necessary? That might be powdered sugar for all you know. I don't see Tory running from you. Why would she have called you and given you permission to check her house if she had drugs in here in plain sight?"

The sergeant thought a moment, his

forehead scrunched, and then proceeded to put the handcuffs on her wrist behind her. "I have to follow procedures. Let's go."

"Jordan, please watch Morgan for me."

"Of course. And I'll call my attorney in Denver. Don't worry about Morgan. We'll get this straightened out."

As Tory was paraded out of her house, Sergeant Bennett at her side, she feared all the neighbors were peeking out their windows. She was innocent of everything the police thought she had done, and the truth should come out. But in this nightmare, logic didn't make any difference. It was as if in this world, the laws were turned inside out.

At the police station, she sat in an interview room with only a table and two chairs while a test was run on the white powder. She prayed that the mess would be straightened out quickly, that she wouldn't lose her job over this, and that Charles Nelson would turn up, alive or dead. *I'm innocent, Lord. Please help me prove it.*

An hour later, the door finally opened,

and an older silver-haired man entered the room. "I'm Police Chief Hoffman."

Good. Someone in authority who'll listen to reason.

After the police chief read the Miranda rights to her, he continued. "Your lawyer is on his way, but why don't you make it easier on yourself and tell us where you got the heroin? It's to your benefit to cooperate with us. I'll make sure the DA knows you have."

Heroin? Heroin! Tory couldn't wrap her mind around the word. "Heroin? You ran the test?"

"At this moment a thorough search of your house is being conducted. If more is found, you'll be charged as a drug dealer."

"I never touched that bag, let alone put it in my bathroom."

"But we found one of your fingerprints on it."

"Impossible." How could that be? Was she going crazy? She actually pinched herself, praying she would wake up from the nightmare.

But Police Chief Hoffman's hard stare

still bore into her.

* * *

After dropping off Morgan at school, Jordan returned to his house and sat down at the computer. He'd been there all morning, tracking down leads to help Tory. Someone—probably Harold London—was discrediting and framing Tory. So Jordan had several options to help prove Tory was innocent. First, that she was right about Charles Nelson's death. Second, that the man in her house left the drugs to set up a frame. Fingerprints could be planted, if someone were determined enough. The night before the break-in, he and Tory had been at Harold's house. Maybe she'd touched something and left her fingerprint.

But how to prove it? He needed to talk to Gage about that.

Helplessness blanketed Jordan. It was too much like that time he'd been buried under rubble after the bomb had exploded and killed so many of his buddies. He kept trying to free himself, but he was trapped, listening to the cries of pain from others in the same situation.

Dutch nudged his arm. He rubbed his dog's fur, and the anxiety began to subside.

For the first time in two years, he felt needed. Tory needed him, and so did Morgan. He had to keep it together for them.

Her son had been stunned when Jordan had told him the day before about what happened to his mother. And to make matters worse her arraignment wouldn't be until the very end of the day, although the lawyer he'd hired for Tory had tried to get that changed.

Coming up with dead ends on the computer, Jordan decided to explore the area around the original crime scene on the mountain road for a body or a fresh grave. Then he wanted to check out the Nelsons' land without them knowing. He couldn't just sit and do nothing while Tory remained in jail.

He grabbed his keys and Dutch's leash, called his dog, and headed to his SUV. As he started the engine, his cell phone rang. It was Gage. "Tell me some good news about the red substance on the leaves."

"It's human blood, but there's not enough to do a DNA test."

"Okay, that might help Tory. What did you find out about Harold London?"

"He and your local police chief, Bob Hoffman, grew up together in Crystal Creek. They were best friends."

"So the police chief could be covering for Harold's son?"

"A possibility. There's been some chatter about a few cases in the last few years concerning Crystal Creek that might not have been on the up-and-up concerning the police. Nothing concrete. Most people feel Harold London is an upstanding citizen. He gives a lot of money to worthy causes in Crystal Creek and the surrounding area. With all the property you own there, I'm surprised you haven't had any dealings with the man."

Jordan turned onto the highway that led to the mountain road. "Because I let my lawyer do all the negotiations for me.

However, I did meet him Tuesday evening. I haven't gotten involved much in what goes on in Crystal Creek."

"But you are now. Why?"

"I don't like people in authority using the system in their favor. Tory doesn't deserve what's happening to her. She reported a crime she witnessed, and now she's the criminal in the eyes of the police. When power is abused, it hurts everyone."

"One rotten apple can spoil the whole basket."

"A man attacked Tory yesterday. He had a switchblade, and I was able to recover it. I gave it to the sergeant on this case. Tory told me one of her fingerprints was found on the plastic bag with heroin the police discovered in her bathroom on the counter."

Gage whistled. "Fingerprints are an important piece of evidence. How well do you know this Tory?"

Jordan ground his teeth. "First, if she had known about the bag of heroin in her bathroom, she would never have agreed to Officer Ward checking the house. Second, I know her and she wouldn't do drugs. She didn't touch the bag. Which leaves me to wonder how can fingerprints be planted."

"It's possible to transfer them if you know how and are careful, but if the lab examines them in detail under a microscope, it should be clear they were planted."

"Good. I'll make sure Tory's lawyer requests that. Any word on the sports car?"

"Not yet, but your police chief had sent out an alert on the car. I asked the surrounding law enforcement agencies to let me know when they notify him."

"Thanks. I'm hoping there's evidence on the car that proves someone was hit."

"Should be. I'll keep digging, and if I find anything, I'll let you know. Watch your step, Jordan. Crystal Creek isn't familiar territory, and if someone is going to the trouble of planting fingerprints, they are serious—and dangerous."

Shortly after Jordan disconnected the cell phone, he headed up the north face of the mountain and stopped about fifty yards beyond where the hit-and-run had occurred, parking in a cutout. As he walked along the shoulder on the ravine side, he looked for a way down. Below, the ground leveled out into relatively flat terrain before dropping off again twenty yards away. Remnants of leftover snow from early last week still littered the area, especially under the evergreen trees.

When he reached the scene, he ruled out the mountainside of the road. It shot straight up and, aside from bighorn sheep, no one went in that direction. About ten yards past the crime scene, Jordan found a way down the side of the steep slope. From the sight of footprints, he wasn't the first person recently who had used the trail. The only way an injured seventy-two year old man ended up in the ravine was if someone carried him or tossed his body into it. Or he fell.

He searched the area, hurrying because he didn't have a lot of time since he had to pick up Morgan at a certain time at school. He set his right foot against a small rock and shifted his weight. The stone broke loose, and Jordan tumbled down the slope, hitting the bottom with a thud. Bruised and cut, he stood and inspected the ground. Ignoring the pain from the fall, he hiked along the small ridge. Nothing. If Charles Nelson fell, he should have found the body or remains of one.

He made his way back up the slope using roots, rocks, and scrubs to haul himself up to the road. He didn't think Nelson was down in the ravine. He'd examined all potential hiding places, but Tory had said she was only gone half an hour to find a phone to call the authorities. No one had time to get down the slope, bury the man, and climb back up.

That meant someone probably came from up the mountain road and took Charles somewhere. He'd go to the top and note where turn offs and houses were. Seeing the time on his clock on the dashboard, he decided he'd have to come back out here tomorrow to investigate the Nelson property.

Between the crime scene and the top, he saw five houses besides the Nelsons' and Josh's family. At the summit, Jordan parked, climbed from his SUV with Dutch and panned the vista. Off to the south, he spied part of the London compound, its high fence a telltale sign. He took out his binoculars and examined it closely. A dirt road led from the back of the property into a dense evergreen forest. Did it come out onto this highway? There must be a way if Peter London were driving the sports car. If there wasn't a road to connect the London property to this highway, Peter must have been visiting one of the people on the north face.

But there was no time to do more. He had to pick up Morgan and get to the courthouse for Tory's arraignment. As he turned around, he glimpsed what he believed might be the exit for the road from the back of the London property. It wasn't in the best of shape, and he wouldn't want to drive a sports car over it, but it could be done. He'd find out tomorrow.

Back in cell phone range, he noticed he had a message. It was the secretary at Morgan's school. Apparently, the boy had been in a fight and would be waiting in the principal's office. Jordan sighed and pushed the SUV beyond the speed limit. He made it to the school only a few minutes early, parked and strode into the building. Morgan sat in the area outside Mr. Mayne's office, slouched in a chair, a frown on his face along with some red, swollen splotches. The kid would have a black eye by tomorrow.

"What happened?" Jordan took the chair next to Morgan.

The boy balled his hands. "Someone called my mom a nut and a druggie. She isn't."

"No, she isn't."

Mr. Mayne opened the door and came out. "He is suspended for tomorrow. He can come back when Christmas break is over." He turned to the boy. "Morgan, if you do this again, you'll be suspended much longer."

"Clay started it." Morgan rose as Jordan did.

"I know, and he's suspended too."

Jordan shook the man's hand. "I'll let

Tory know."

Mr. Mayne pinched his lips together as though he wanted to say something. Instead, he returned to his office.

Jordan clasped Morgan's shoulder. "Let's go."

Jordan parked the car on the street in front of the imposing red brick building and hurried with Morgan toward the courtroom. When they went inside, Tory stood next to her lawyer in front of the judge and entered a not guilty plea. Her shoulders sagged when the bond amount of ten thousand was announced.

"Wait here." Jordan caught the attention of the lawyer, Mark Sutton, and said, "I'll take care of it. Tell her she'll be out right away."

Mark nodded and went back to talk with Tory before she was led off. The past twenty-four hours had placed a heavy toll on her. He doubted she'd gotten any sleep last night in her cell. All he wanted to do was hold her and let her know she wasn't alone. His determination to get to the bottom of this strengthened even more.

Someone intended to take her down, and he wasn't going to let him.

FIVE

Tory sat at Jordan's kitchen table and sipped her hot tea, relishing its soothing taste and a moment of quiet after the twenty-four hours she'd spent at the jail. She still couldn't believe it—arrested for possession of heroin. She didn't drink alcohol, let alone take drugs not prescribed for her. If only she could hide and forget that she faced a charge of possession of an illegal drug.

"I'm glad you decided to stay here tonight." Jordan sat beside her. He'd spent an hour clearing out his spare bedroom and blowing up an air mattress while Tory watched him silently. Morgan had already crashed, and Tory would join him soon.

She rubbed her hands up and down her arms as though that would warm her. She'd felt chilled to the bone ever since the man had attacked her, and sleeping in a cell had proved impossible. Every groan, cry, and noise she'd heard amplified her fear—until she began reciting Psalm Twenty-Three. She knew the Lord was with her the whole time, protecting her. "I love my little house. I'd really come to feel at home there. But after yesterday, I don't know if I can go back. At least not until we find out what's going on and that man is caught."

Jordan covered her hand with his. "You can stay as long as you need. I feel better that you're here. Dutch and I will protect you two."

The steel in Jordan's voice reassured Tory. In jail last night, she'd felt so alone. But knowing God was with her and what Jordan had done so far for her had given her peace to at least relax in the early hours of a new day.

"Thank you for putting up my bail. I

can't believe it was so much. If it hadn't been for you, I'd still be there. I don't have that kind of money."

"Which makes me wonder if someone knew that and tried to keep you locked up." Jordan sipped his coffee. "What did Mr. Mayne tell you when you called?"

"Nothing will be done until after the Christmas break, but it doesn't sound good for me. There have been lots of comments from concerned parents, but at the end, he told me quite a few of the parents with children in my class called to show their support. That took the sting out of it. Remind me after this is over never to witness another crime."

"I have a feeling if you did, you'd still do the right thing, even after all of this. You're that kind of person."

His words filled her with a sense of validation and left a glow in its wake. "That's a compliment I appreciate after the horrendous day I've had."

"Tomorrow, I'm going to scout out the Nelsons' place and then check out a dirt road at the top of the mountain that I discovered. I think it leads to the back of the London property. I didn't have time to follow it today because I needed to pick up Morgan."

"I'm coming, too."

"No. I don't want to have to worry about keeping you or Morgan safe."

She shook her head. "I can't let you do all the work when I'm the one trying to prove my innocence."

"We need to dig into the backgrounds of the residents who live on the northern face. My gut tells me someone up the mountain took Charles Nelson's body. You can do that on my computer while I'm gone."

"Josh's mother, Alana, might be able to help with that. She works from home, and they've lived there for years."

"Any tie to London or the police chief? Does Josh's dad work for either one?"

"No, Luke commutes to Denver."

"Good, that might be to our benefit. Call and talk to her about it tomorrow."

She stared at her cup of tea, the color reminding her of Jordan's eyes. What if she hadn't known him? She would have been dealing with all of this alone. She could have managed it, but it felt good to have a person care. With a long sigh, she lifted her mug and finished the rest of the warm tea. "I should go to bed. I hope I can sleep, because my brain is barely functioning. I need rest."

"Sleep in. I'll probably be gone by the time you get up."

Tory rose and took her cup to the sink. "Sleeping in sounds wonderful, but I don't think I'll be doing much of that until this ordeal is over with."

He pushed to his feet. "We had one piece of good news. The blood on the shrub at the crime scene was human. I hope tomorrow to find Charles Nelson's body, and maybe we'll hear something about the fingerprints on your attacker's knife."

"If there were any." Tory strolled toward the hallway, stopped halfway there, and swept around. "I've been trying to figure out how to get my description of the driver down on paper." Her feeble attempts had produced nothing recognizable. "Alana writes children stories, and she draws beautiful pictures for them. She might be able to draw the driver. The photos of Peter I've seen look similar, but something doesn't fit."

"It was nearly dark, and you just got a glimpse, right? He might have been driving close behind you, but there were two windshields between you."

"True. And with the light that time of day, there was quite a glare. I'm sure he had light blond hair, but in all the photos of Peter I've seen, his is dark brown. That might be what's bothering me. I'm beginning to question everything."

"People can change hair color."

"What if someone stole his car, and we're looking at the wrong person?"

"That could be. There are a lot of people out looking for the sports car. Finding it could answer that question." Jordan closed the space between them.

"I'm going to ask Alana to stop by here on the way to pick up Josh at school. Maybe she can do a decent drawing of the guy I saw behind the wheel."

"That's a good idea. I'm leaving Dutch

with you. Just don't leave the house. My alarm system is top notch. If the person in your house on Wednesday was there to frame you, he's accomplished what he wanted to do, so you should be fine. He probably came after you because you surprised him, and he needed to get away." He clasped her hand and tugged her closer. "I'd rather not leave you, but we aren't going to find the answers just by working from here."

"I think you're right."

A look crossed his features—frustration maybe.

"What is it?"

"I can't stop thinking of Bart Nelson's overreaction to our visit. What is he hiding? What if he comes here while I'm gone?"

"I'll be fine. I'm not defenseless. After my husband died, I took defense classes and did quite well. Besides, Dutch will be here. I won't be surprised this time."

"So I need to be wary of you and your expertise."

She laughed. "Hardly. It was nothing like what you went through to be a Navy

SEAL."

The second she said the last two words a frown descended over his features. "Training doesn't prepare you for some things."

"Did something happen to you while serving our country?"

He stepped back, dropping her hand. "Not important."

Hardly, if his expression and tone of voice were any indication. "What happened?" She wanted to know the good and the bad about Jordan.

"You should get some sleep."

"That isn't going to happen, not when you evade my question. My mind probably will spend all night conjuring up all kinds of scenarios. Do you want to be responsible for that?" Her attempt at humor fell flat as the pain in his eyes twisted her heart. "On second thought, forget the question. You don't owe me an explanation."

He took her hand and pulled her toward the den. After she sat on the couch, he moved away and paced. "You might as well get comfortable while I tell you. I haven't told anyone in the States except this counselor I saw the first year I was back here."

Dutch came into the den and sat down in Jordan's path. He squatted and scratched his dog behind the ear. "First off, Dutch isn't an ordinary dog. He's a service dog for people with PTSD. He has an uncanny ability to sense when I get stressed, even if he's in the other room."

"Post-traumatic stress disorder?"

He nodded. "My unit in Afghanistan was ambushed and forced to retreat to a building. It was a set up. The place was wired with bombs that all went off at the same time. Four of us survived and were found hours later under the rubble. Most died instantly, but some didn't, and their cries of suffering will haunt me forever. I was injured and sent back to the States. My tour was almost over. I didn't reenlist."

Tory approached Jordan and knelt next to him. "I'm so sorry. No wonder you have PTSD."

"Before the ambush, I'd seen many horrific acts, but that last one got me. I was near a friend and couldn't get to him to help him. I was pinned down, unable to move. He was suffering and begging me to kill him. His wife had just had their first baby. Her name was the last thing he said after hours of agony. No matter how much I try, I can't shake that off. I couldn't put it in a box and lock it away like I had everything else that happened over there. It broke me."

His pain inundated her as though it were her own. She wanted to draw him into her embrace and help him forget the horrors of war, but before she could, he shot to his feet.

"I shouldn't have said anything. It's the past, and I'm learning to deal with it."

When she rose, she cupped his face. "Thank you for telling me. I've always found the more I talk about a painful situation, the less it hurts. No matter how much we want to forget, we can't until we deal with it. In my case, the grief over my husband's death. There was a time I was so angry with him for dying and leaving me alone. Maybe some of your feelings are wrapped up in survivor's guilt."

"The first six months after I got back, I denied anything was wrong. Then one day I lost it and nearly destroyed my house in my rage. So many lives destroyed that day. It scared me enough to seek out counseling. Before that, I'd refused all offers to talk about what happened."

"But you did finally get help. That's what is important. Some people don't. They don't want to accept that something is wrong. When a traumatic event happens in a person's life, that will leave a mark." Tory hugged Jordan, hoping to convey her support as he had supported her.

He wound his arms around her and held her against him. "I've learned life is precious. I've learned to depend on the Lord. He'll walk with you even through the dark."

She leaned back slightly and stared up into Jordan's face. "I know. He was with me in jail last night."

Jordan's tender look underscored her growing feelings toward him. His fingers delved into her hair, and he angled his head and lowered it toward her. She welcomed the touch of his lips against hers. The gentle possession drove all thoughts of the past from Tory. Nothing else mattered but this moment.

Until the phone rang, breaking them apart.

Jordan hurried to the end table next to the couch to answer it. "Hello."

As he listened to the person on the other end, Jordan's brow creased, and his eyes became solemn.

"Thanks, Gage. I'll let Tory know." Jordan replaced the receiver in its cradle and turned to her. "They found the black sports car. It crashed and burned outside Denver. Gage just came back from the scene. If there had been any forensic evidence, it's gone now."

Her heart sank. The *stolen* vehicle wouldn't back up her story. "Other than the human blood on the foliage, there isn't anything to collaborate what I witnessed."

"There is Charles Nelson's body. It's somewhere, and I intend to find it."

* * *

Jordan parked his SUV off the mountain road and hiked toward the Nelson property. He hoped to search the area and see if he could find any signs of a fresh grave. Although Bart Nelson didn't seem too smart, Jordan doubted he would have stashed his dad's body near his house, especially because of the smell. He would have to have found a way to mask the odor. It can be done but not easily. But outside in the surrounding woods on his land, if he was buried in the ground, the smell wouldn't be as evident.

Then if he had time, Jordan still wanted to check out that road coming from the back of the London's estate. He might be able to persuade the police to investigate, since the car had been reported stolen. He could use its discovery to press the point that Tory had seen a hit-and-run and was being framed on the drug charge by the driver of the sports car. In his gut, he still thought it had been Peter London driving that day. Would Sergeant Bennett listen to logic and reason? He didn't know if the man was on the London payroll or not, but he didn't like how this all had been handled by the police. Someone wanted to discredit Tory. Harold London? The police chief and Harold's friend? Another police officer?

Or somehow, Bart Nelson?

With his backpack on, Jordan made his way through the evergreen forest between the road and the Nelsons' house, slowly combing the area for any sign of a grave. Occasionally, he used his binoculars to scan the ground around him. As he grew closer to the dilapidated house where Bart had confronted them with a rifle, Jordan ran through several scenarios of what might have happened that day.

If he were Bart and had carried Charles Nelson from the site of the hit-and-run, intending to bury him, the woods would be a good place to dig a grave. It would be easy to scatter debris over the spot of freshly dug ground and hide it. With his binoculars, Jordan inspected the forest floor. Why would the son cover up the death of his own father? Why wouldn't he just leave his father to be found by the police? The sight of a slight bump in the flat ground with pine needles and dead leaves strewn over it made Jordan pause. Could that be the grave or an answer his imagination had conjured up?

He started to move toward the place in question, but the hairs on the back of his neck tingled. Jordan stopped and rotated in a circle. He froze when he spied Bart standing a few yards away.

Bart's rifle was aimed at Jordan's chest.

* * *

Tory's head pulsated with tension, the pain mounting. Her eyes stung from staring at the computer screen for hours, but she finally thought she had a complete list of all the people who lived on the north side of the mountain. She wasn't sure how helpful it would be. When Alana came in a couple of hours, she could start questioning her about her neighbors. Alana might be able to give her insight into them that a computer couldn't tell her.

But could she really trust Alana? How well did she know Josh's mother? Only through her son and the occasional conversation they'd had, usually involving their children. What if Alana or her husband had a tie to Harold London somehow? Her name was on the short list of homeowners who lived on the mountain's north face.

Tory bowed her head, closing her eyes, and tried to copy the massage that Jordan had given her the other day. But her kneading wasn't deep enough to work the stress from her neck.

"Mom, there's a cop car in our driveway," Morgan shouted from the front bedroom.

She closed the laptop and jumped to her feet. Hurrying toward Morgan, she said, "Shh. Quiet."

Not that she was hiding from the police, but she had no reason to trust them. There were only two people who could have planted that heroin in her bathroom—Officer Wade and the intruder.

"Get back from the window," Tory snapped as she entered the bedroom she and her son were using.

"He went to our front door. Now he's looking in the garage window."

"Get back. Now."

Morgan let go of the blind slat and swung around. "Maybe he has some good news. You said the car was found last night. What if there was evidence to prove what you saw?"

Those were possibilities. It was also possible the officer knew Jordan was gone and decided to take care of her. Okay, maybe she was becoming paranoid, but could anyone blame her after the past week?

"Then we'll find out when Jordan gets back."

Sounds of barking and growling came from the foyer.

"Stay here." She shoved her cell phone into her son's hands. "Call 911 if someone breaks in. Wait no. That might not be good." As Dutch continued to yelp, she found Morgan's backpack, tore a piece of paper out of his notebook, and wrote down a number. "Call Jordan's police friend,

Gage, in Denver. Let him know what's going on."

Her heartbeat pounding against her chest, she crept toward the living room, hoping whoever was out there would go away. As she passed the front door, the doorbell rang. She gasped. Her pulse raced as she waited. It rang again.

Dutch stood in front of the door and barked as though he would tear anyone to pieces who came inside.

There was no way the officer could know she was inside. If she were quiet, the cop would go away—at least that's what she prayed.

When she headed for the front window, she heard the screen door opening, and she stopped and glanced back into the foyer. Suddenly a pounding against the wood sent fear to every part of her. What would the police do next? Break in? She frantically looked around for a place to hide. Maybe she'd fit behind the couch.

"Mom?" her son's whispered voice penetrated the haze of panic trying to take hold of her.

She hastened into the foyer and motioned for Morgan to join her. She put her forefinger over her lips, grabbed him, and pulled him to the couch. "Hide behind here."

"Mrs. Caldwell?" A voice called through the door. "Your neighbor said you were in here. I need to talk to you. It's urgent."

She couldn't forget Sergeant Bennett's husky voice. He was here. Wanting her to open the door. Her body quaked as she strode to the blinds covering the living room window. Was more than one police officer with him? What was so urgent? Did something happen to Jordan? She remembered the rifle Bart Nelson had fired when they'd left his house.

Please, God, don't let anything happen to Jordan. He was only trying to help me.

"Mrs. Caldwell, please open. You could be in danger." A plea rang through the sergeant's words.

He hadn't believed her story from the beginning. He'd suspected her of using drugs and lying. Because of him, she had been handcuffed, led from her house, and locked in a jail cell overnight. The memory sent a quaver through her.

"Please. There might not be much time."

Whom did she trust?

The Lord.

What do I do?

Open the door.

She took one step toward the foyer and stopped. She tried to lift her foot to move forward, but it felt rooted to the floor.

"The Nelsons are dead."

SIX

Arms spread-eagled in the Nelsons' shed, feet bound and mouth gagged, Jordan hung from the rafters like a side of beef. Through the slits between the two-by-fours that comprised the walls, he'd seen Bart and his wife loading their possessions into a brand new Ford Explorer. Then the doors slammed, and they drove away.

How long would they be gone? A few hours? Days? Would they leave him here to die?

The wife had been furious with Bart about what he'd done. Jordan still hadn't quite figured out what it was that Bart had done. Did he bury his father? Did he somehow plan his dad's death? He couldn't imagine Bart orchestrating the theft of the sports car from the London compound, and from what Tory described of the driver, it certainly hadn't been Bart who hit his father. According to Jordan's research, only Bart, his wife, and his father had lived here.

Jordan couldn't help wondering where the money to buy a new car had come from. Based on the condition of his homestead, Bart didn't have a lot of cash. Had Harold London paid him off? Or maybe Bart's dad had stashed away some money?

Jordan's arms felt like they were being pulled from their sockets. His head throbbed with pain. Bart, a man of few words, had forced Jordan with a gun aimed at him to enter the shed and kneel. The man kept his distance so Jordan didn't have an opportunity to overpower him without being shot. After he got down on his knees, Jordan waited, trying to figure out what he could do. Suddenly he was struck from behind with something like a shovel. He tumbled to the dirt floor, blackness swallowing him.

The hammering inside his skull and Bart's wife yelling had aroused him from unconsciousness.

He had to figure out a way to get loose. He didn't want Tory coming after him. What if the Nelsons came back and captured her, too?

Jordan surveyed the small shed. Piles of tools he couldn't reach sat beside boxes stacked along two walls. He peered at the rope cutting into his wrists. His hands were numb. It was hard to swing his body with his legs tied together. The only way out of this that he could see, short of being rescued, would be to pull the rafter down and pray it didn't hit him on its way to the floor. He studied the thick beam and, sure enough, there were plenty of signs of rotting wood. Maybe he could get it to split.

With all his might, he swayed from one side to the other, using his momentum to pull on his arm. Pain knifed through him each time he jerked on the rope.

The wood creaked in protest. With two

more swings of his body, the rafter beam snapped and came crashing down on top of him.

* * *

It's a trap. Those words screamed through Tory's thoughts as she crept toward the front door at Jordan's house. She'd just commanded Dutch to stay by her son, so she was on her own.

Her hand shook so much she could hardly grip the doorknob. What if the sergeant was here to help? If the Nelsons were dead, was Jordan dead, too? He'd been heading to their property.

With her hand on the knob, she glanced toward the couch and whispered, "Morgan, I need to talk with the officer. You stay hidden until I tell you to come out."

She turned the doorknob and pulled the door open, but only enough for her to wedge her body into the gap, blocking the sergeant from coming inside. Not that she was kidding herself. If the man wanted in, he could overpower her.

Every cell of her body was on heightened alert as she looked up into the sergeant's solemn expression. "What happened to the Nelsons?"

"They went off the road not far from where you reported the hit-and-run. Not sure about what caused it, but they landed in the ravine. When I got there, Bart Nelson was still alive. He kept mumbling, 'London did it'."

"Did what? The hit-and-run?"

The sergeant shrugged. "I'm not sure. He didn't say anything else. Officer Ward got to the scene before I did and..." He scowled and averted his gaze.

"Are you two partners or something? He was at the hit-and-run scene, my house and now the Nelsons' wreck."

"I never worked with him much until lately."

"Did Bart say something to Officer Ward before you got there?"

"Ward says no, but I saw Nelson's lips moving. I'd just arrived and came down the ravine. I hurried to hear what he said, but he died seconds before I got to him."

Tory sidestepped to allow the sergeant into the house. "What aren't you telling me?"

"I was coming to see you when the call came over the radio about the wreck. I detoured and went to that scene. I thought I had a good chance to be first because I was close. Somehow Officer Ward was there before me. Seems he must've been on that road to begin with. I asked him where he came from. He said there'd been a call about hearing gunfire. On the way here to talk to you, I checked with dispatch. There wasn't any call like that."

"You think the officer had something to do with the wreck?" She glanced toward Dutch to make sure he was still in place. She didn't know what to believe or who to trust.

"I don't know. Something doesn't feel right about this past week."

"What do you mean?" She closed the front door. She knew nothing had been right except a man was killed and she was attacked.

"Officer Ward took the blood on the

road to the lab to be tested. He offered, because I was going to go to the London residence first. I never thought anything about it until I started thinking about your call to 911 when you were attacked. I responded. Officer Ward insisted he should back me up. Again, not strange by itself, but every time something connected with that original call from you about the hit-and-run came in, he's been nearby. That's never happened before." Frowning, he rubbed his nape.

"I'm innocent of the drug charge. There are only two people who could have planted the drugs in the bathroom—my attacker and Officer Ward."

The lines of his scowl deepened. "That's what I was thinking, if you were innocent like you said. I received a call from a detective in Denver, apparently a friend of Mr. Steele's, last night. He told me they found the sports car. When I met him at the scene of that accident, he told me you two had found blood on a shrub near the site of the hit-and-run. I guess you heard the blood on the shrub was human."

She nodded. "Yeah, we heard that last night."

"Well, so this morning I talked with the lab technician who processed the blood on the road. There was an hour gap from when Officer Ward should have been at the lab and when he turned in the evidence. That was odd, since he insisted because we'd run the license plate HOTSHOT and knew it was Peter London's car that it was necessary to get the blood to the lab right away. Harold London has done a lot for the town and is powerful. He would want answers. Then, on top of all of that, when I called Charles's brother to see if I could get hold of him, the man answered and told me Charles didn't go with him this year."

"So you finally believe me?"

"I think so, ma'am. Sorry about...well, all of it." The sergeant stared at his feet for a moment, seemed to be waiting for her to say something.

She took a deep breath. "What's done is done."

He looked up and half-smiled. "Thanks." He peered past her into the living room.

"Where's Mr. Steele? He may be in danger too."

Had the sergeant been lying and wanted to make sure Jordan wasn't here before he did something to her? She backed a few steps toward Dutch. "Why do you think Jordan is in danger?"

"Like I said, something doesn't fit. I'm not sure who to trust. I know the chief is a good friend of Harold London. Although I've never doubted the chief's integrity before, I'm not sure what's going on. But if someone killed the Nelson family because of the hit-and-run, then I would guess you're a target too. And after you were attacked this week, well, that seems pretty obvious. And since Steele is helping you, he might be making himself a target."

She crossed her arms. "I don't even know if I can trust you."

"I don't blame you. This morning, I did some checking with Nelson's neighbors. One of them told me the old man walked every day about the time you reported the hit-and-run. Nelson told me his father wouldn't have been on that road. Another inconsistency in this case."

Lord, I'm in Your hands. "Jordan went to the Nelson property to look for Charles Nelson's grave. We thought Bart might have carried him back there."

"If Bart found his father's body, then why did he lie about his father's whereabouts?"

"I don't know."

"I was on the way to interview Nelson again when the call about the wreck came in."

What if the Nelsons fled because they killed Jordan or hurt him? The man was quick to shoot. Although Jordan had been trained to take care of himself, it's hard to outrun a bullet. Chills encased her. "Why did the Nelsons leave?"

"They had a brand new car packed with their belongings. Something might have spooked them."

"We need to go to the Nelsons' place."

"I agree. Where's your son?"

Until this, she'd never had trouble trusting before. Certainly she'd never doubted people in authority, but after everything that had happened in the previous week, her trust had been stretched beyond the limit.

But now, with the sergeant on her side, it seemed she'd be able to prove her innocence, and they'd discover what had happened to that poor old man. God hadn't let her down yet, and she had to believe He was looking out for her. "Morgan, come out. We're going with Sergeant Bennett."

Her son crawled from behind the couch and stood by Jordan's dog. "Can we take Dutch?"

"Yes," she said while the sergeant shook his head. She turned to Sergeant Bennett. "If Jordan is hurt somewhere on that property, Dutch will be able to find him. We're not going without the dog."

"You're not going with me. I'm going to take you to the station and go alone."

"Forget it. You said yourself you don't know who to trust. We do this together, or I go alone." She lifted her chin and hoped all her resolve showed in her expression.

His lips turned down at the corners. His eyes narrowed as he studied her. After a moment, he sighed. "Fine, but you need to do what I say. This is against police procedure."

"This whole situation seems riddled with procedures that have gone against police policy."

For the first time, she glimpsed the sergeant's grin. "True. And I aim to rectify that. Let's go."

She, Morgan, Sergeant Bennett, and Dutch stepped out of Jordan's front door. As she turned to make sure it was locked, she breathed a prayer.

Please let him be alive.

* * *

Pain pierced through the haze blanketing Jordan's mind. He tried to move and couldn't. He forced his eyes open and shifted to see what was holding him in place. Through the gaps in the debris covering him, Jordan saw a beam had fallen on top of the rubble. Dust clouded the air, and he coughed.

With his sore body, he shoved at boxes

and boards, pushing them off of his body. The effort drained him, and he fell back onto the dirt floor.

He struggled to breathe as memories of Afghanistan flooded his mind. Hurled back two years, he felt the weight of that distant building pinning him down. He heard the barrage of bullets and cries for help. He smelled the blood, dust and gunpowder. The pressure on his chest threatened to rob him of any air.

No!

I'm not going there.

I'm in Colorado.

He fixed on the image of Tory with her beautiful smile. She was real.

God is with me, just like He had been that day.

One shallow breath grew deeper as he focused on calming himself. Then another. Tory was at his house, waiting for him. Again he pulled much-needed air into his lungs.

When he had regained control, he heaved the debris off him one piece at a time. One arm was pinned down, but the other was free enough that he could use it to shove the pieces of wood from his chest and legs. He had no choice. The Nelsons could come back. Worse yet, they could go after Tory and Morgan.

* * *

"Jordan was going to hike through the woods. He was looking for a possible gravesite for Charles Nelson." Tory spied Jordan's SUV through some vegetation along the mountain road. "His car is over there." She pointed out the side window of the police cruiser.

Sergeant Bennett pulled onto the shoulder and then across the rough terrain to park. "Let's go in on foot. Use Dutch. He might be able to follow his owner's scent."

"Mom, can I hold his leash? I won't let go."

"That's okay with me." Then to the sergeant she added, "Morgan has walked Dutch some on the leash, so the dog is used to him."

"Let's go. The family is gone so we

should be all right. We stay together, and if I tell you to hide or do something, do it, no question." The officer opened his trunk and took out a shotgun.

Morgan's eyes grew round as he eyed the firearm in the man's holster and the larger gun now propped against his shoulder.

"Never hurts to be prepared," Bennett said.

Tory patted her son's back. "Stay next to me. And remember to do what Sergeant Bennett says." On the ride to the Nelsons' place, her anxiety had eased about trusting the sergeant. Whoever had planted the heroin in her house had meant business, and she was glad the sergeant finally believed her.

"We'll let Dutch lead us, so give him a long leash." The sergeant joined them. "By the way, after all that's happened, please call me Kevin. I figure we're in this together."

She slanted a smile at him. "Thanks for finally believing me."

Dutch must have picked up Jordan's

trail, because the dog crisscrossed through the woods as though searching for something.

Tory scanned the area for any sign of Jordan. "We believe Bart came to the hit-and-run site and took his dad's body away."

"Why would he do that?"

"Not sure. But I know what I saw, and a dead man doesn't walk, so someone had to take Charles Nelson's body in that thirty-minute time frame. I didn't see a car go by me on my way down to the store nor one on the way back up. I kept an eye on the road, because I wanted to make sure I didn't miss you all. When I went to the restroom for a few minutes, I asked the clerk to watch for me. He told me no one had driven past either way."

"He could have lied."

"I gave him a tip, and he knew I was watching for the police. The logical answer was that someone came down the road and took the body. It was getting dark and maybe Bart got worried about his father being out on the road. That isn't a safe place to be in the dark without a flashlight."

"From what little I know about Bart Nelson, I would think he'd want justice for his father."

"Maybe instead, he blackmailed someone to keep quiet about his father's death. He could have witnessed it as he came out of his property and knew who was driving. I was too busy looking at the car behind me. I didn't look at the side of the road. Justice wouldn't bring his dad back. Money might have allowed Bart to buy that new car. The Nelsons might have used some money to go on a vacation, and that's where they were going today." Dutch stopped and sniffed the ground, so Tory paused and waited to see which way the dog would go next.

"And you still think Peter London was driving?"

"The guy I saw looks similar to him, but I haven't seen him in person. In all the pictures I've seen of Peter, he has dark hair. The driver was light blond."

"When I met with him and his father, Peter had bleached his hair at school.

Apparently, he lost a bet the day before."

She'd realized hair color could be changed but hadn't known it had been. The more she thought about it that had been the only thing that had concerned her about the driver. "Then, yes, I think he was driving his car." As Dutch moved forward, Tory did too.

When they neared the edge of the forest, Tory glimpsed a movement at far side of the house. "Someone is at the Nelsons' place, and I don't think it's Jordan. Not big enough."

Kevin stared to the left of the home. "Yeah, and I see another one. I recognize that guy. He works for Harold London. It looks like him and his buddy are breaking into the house. You two stay back while I secure them. Don't come out until I tell you. If something happens to me, get help." He handed her the keys to his car.

After the sergeant left, Tory put her son behind her against a tree and held onto Dutch's leash. She peeked around the tree to watch just as Kevin glanced into the front window. He went around back and disappeared. Every nerve was stretched taut in the silence of the forest. She wished she'd left Morgan with Mrs. Scott, but she had been so worried whoever was behind all of this would come after her and her son. Were the men looking for the dead body? Or something else?

Jordan's dog emitted a low growl that sent goose bumps up her arms.

"Quiet, Dutch. We can't let them know we're here."

Pacing, the dog growled louder and louder. Tory began a sweep of the area, but before she could scout the woods behind her, Dutch charged in that direction, straining against the leash, a ferocious look on his face.

Tory held the leash and peered around the trunk of the tree. Two men, armed, stalked toward them. One aimed his gun toward the dog while the other pointed his revolver at her.

"Lady, if you don't control that animal, I'll kill it."

The savagery in his voice and those piercing blue eyes—she would never forget them. Nor would she forget the feel of that man's hands cutting off her air just a few days earlier. He would kill her—kill her son, too, if she didn't do as he said. She gripped the leash until her hand hurt, tugging the hundred-pound German shepherd toward her.

"Tie him to the tree." Blue Eyes indicated one about five yards away.

"You're such a softie when it comes to dogs." His partner chuckled.

"If we shoot him, it'll alert that guy we saw going into the house. We need to surprise him."

Once Tory had the dog tied up, she knelt by the German shepherd and said, "Please boy. Stay quiet. If you make any noise, they'll shoot you."

When she rose, Blue Eyes gestured for her to join them. His partner plastered Morgan against his front and held a gun to his head. With all that had happened lately, this was the worst. The terror on her son's face pained her more than anything. They had only come to find Jordan and a safe place to hide until the sergeant tracked down some leads. How could she have known these men would show up at the Nelsons' place? All she'd wanted was to keep Morgan safe, and now her precious child had a gun to his head. With the couple dead from the car accident, the Nelsons weren't a threat anymore to whoever was behind all of this. Would she end up like them?

"Morgan, do as they say."

"Smart lady." Blue eyes yanked her toward him and captured her against him. The feel of his hands, the scent of his skin, only amplified the memories of that terrifying attack. Her pulse rate kicked up a notch, and sweat popped out on her forehead.

The men hauled Tory and her son toward the house.

Where was Jordan? She scanned the yard and noticed that part of the shed had collapsed since they'd visited the Nelsons on Sunday. Was Jordan searching another part of the property? He was their only chance—assuming he wasn't hurt or worse.

* * *

Sore and bruised, but free to move around, Jordan lay hidden among the shed debris. He'd seen the sergeant enter the Nelsons' house and hadn't revealed his location. Why was he here? Helping those two men inside?

Jordan needed to leave before the three decided to check the shed. He could get Tory and Morgan and take them to Denver. Gage could help him, because if the sergeant was in on this, then he didn't know whom to trust on the local police force. Certainly not the chief, who could be behind everything to help protect his friend. Jordan prayed Tory and Morgan were safe.

Out of the corner of his eye, he caught a movement at the edge of the forest. Two large goons were holding Tory and Morgan captive, guns to their heads. Rage flashed down Jordan's body. He imagined running toward them to free them. He forced himself to stop, take a deep breath. Patience could be the best strategy for a warrior in certain circumstances. He'd have to pick them off one by one.

When the four disappeared inside by the back door, Jordan dashed to the side of the house and stopped under a window to try and see what was going on in there. He peered into what must be the living room.

Two men sat on the couch with their arms behind their backs. Standing in front of them, the sergeant glanced toward the rear of the house and frowned. It looked like the sergeant had taken the first two men captive. Maybe he wasn't working for whoever was behind this whole mess.

Sergeant Bennett stepped back, dropped his gun, and raised his hands. The two men came into the room, pushing Tory and Morgan in front of them, still holding guns to their heads. The boy was crying, tears streaking down his face. Although a pasty white, Tory looked furious.

While the sergeant started freeing the guys on the couch, Jordan hurried around the side of the house to the door, hoping it wasn't locked. He inched it open and squeezed through the gap into the kitchen.

"You two continue your search of the woods," one of the men said. "Once these three are tied up, we'll finish looking in here, then the shed. Maybe Nelson buried his father under all that rubble."

Another asked, "Why not shoot them now?"

Jordan tensed.

"Not without the boss's okay," the first guy replied. "Let's do the job we came for. That's our priority. We don't know where Steele is."

The sound of the front door opening and closing drew Jordan into the hallway. Two-to-one were good odds for him. After he took care of these two, he'd go after the others.

He heard someone coming. He ducked into some kind of storage room across from the kitchen.

Jordan waited, listening to the footsteps on the wooden floor. The man paused in the hallway just outside the storage room. His body aching, Jordan clenched his hands, ignoring the pain and preparing himself to do what was necessary. The person moved away from him. He relaxed his tense stance and started for the door when the man returned to the hallway. The knob turned.

* * *

As soon as the two men left the room, Tory whispered to her son, "Are you all right? Did they hurt you?"

"No. What if they do something to Dutch?"

"He'll be okay. We're in the Lord's hands, and He'll protect us." She leaned over and kissed the top of her son's head. "I love you."

"I love you, Mom."

While the two men searched the house, Tory fought to loosen the rope around her wrists. She had a better chance than Kevin, who was handcuffed. She scooted around. "See if you can help me while they're gone."

The sergeant put his back to hers and fumbled with the cord. When one of the men came toward the room, Tory and

Kevin sat forward on the couch. The guy glared at them and headed up the stairs. When he disappeared from view, she twisted so Kevin could continue helping her with the rope. She heard a thump against the floor coming from the rear of the house. Surely Charles Nelson wasn't hidden in the house. What were they looking for?

Another two minutes, and she was free. She quickly turned to Morgan and untied him. While he worked on the cord around his feet, Tory released Kevin's bound feet and hers. "Let try to get out of here."

"We'll go out the front and hope the other two are deep in the woods by now. I suggest we run west. The cover is closer that way." With his wrists still handcuffed, Kevin struggled to stand.

As Tory and Morgan rose, a gravelly voice from the staircase said, "You aren't going anywhere." The man descended the steps, his gun directed at them. "Sit before my patience runs out. It's obvious we can't leave you alone." He positioned himself in the entrance to a small dining room that led to the kitchen and yelled, "Bobby Joe, I need your help."

If only she'd worked faster. According to Kevin, one of the men worked for the London family, which meant they might kill them to keep that fact a secret. Ice flowed through her veins. She sent up another prayer.

* * *

When someone shouted for Bobby Joe, the man who had been charging toward Jordan hesitated and looked toward the door. Jordan lowered his shoulder and barreled into the guy, sending him back against a stack of crates. The impact stunned the guy long enough for Jordan to punch him in his gut, then finish him off with an upper cut.

"Bobby Joe, where are you? Did you find something?"

Jordan half expected the man to come looking for his cohort. He opened the door a few inches and peered into the hallway. No one was there. When he left the storage room, he checked the hallway into the foyer. Clear. He hurried down the corridor and sneaked toward the living room. He spied Tory and Morgan sitting at one end of the couch, fear in their eyes. Where was the sergeant?

A man with a gun moved toward the couch, waving the weapon at Tory. "Tie up your son, then the officer."

Somehow Tory was free. No wonder the man didn't come looking for his cohort.

When she stooped in front of Morgan to put the rope around his feet, the gunman shouted, "Bobby Joe, so help me—"

Before the man could turn, Jordan plowed into him, sending him flying toward Sergeant Bennett, who was seated in a chair on the opposite side of the room with his hands behind his back. The officer kicked the assailant in his stomach.

Jordan focused on getting the gun. When the guy tried to suck in air, Jordan brought down his fisted hands like a sledgehammer, onto the gunman's nape, then snatched the revolver from his loosened grip. As the assailant fell, the sergeant finished him off by kneeing him in the head.

"Where's the other one?" the sergeant asked.

"Out cold in the storeroom. I need to take care of him before he wakes up."

"Go. I've got this one." The police officer glared down at the man. "Tory, will you search for the keys to the handcuffs? He pocketed them."

Jordan grabbed some rope on the floor and headed for the back. After he trussed up Bobby Joe and took his weapon, he dragged the guy into the living room to find the sergeant free of his handcuffs and helping Tory tie up the other guy.

"Now all we have to do is take care of the two in the woods," Jordan said to the sergeant.

"Are you sure you're up for it? What happened to you?" Sergeant Bennett took the gun off the downed man he and Tory had secured.

"I pulled the shed down to free myself."

The sergeant eyed the weapon in Jordan's hands. "You know how to use that?"

"I was a Navy SEAL. I served ten years." He turned to Tory. "Will you two be okay by yourselves?"

"Don't worry about Morgan and me. I'll take care of my son. You take care of the rest of them."

As Jordan stepped onto the porch, Tory added, "The guy with blue eyes is the one who attacked me in my house. I won't forget those eyes."

Tory stood at the window and watched them disappear into the trees. *Please, Lord, keep them safe.*

She switched her attention between the view outside and to the guys who were tied up. She kept her hand on Morgan's shoulder. The connection made her feel everything would be all right, as though God was reassuring her they would be safe.

* * *

Jordan pointed at the two men in the woods about twenty yards ahead of them, so focused on the terrain and looking for the gravesite that he hoped they wouldn't know what hit them until it was too late. Earlier when he'd seen Dutch leashed to a tree, he'd unhooked his dog and signaled the German shepherd to follow.

Now, he sent Dutch to the right through the underbrush while he and the sergeant flanked to the left. With his dog in place to move in on the two assailants as a distraction, Jordan lifted his arm in the air as if he were going to throw a rope at a fleeing calf and indicated the German shepherd charge.

Dutch flew out of the brush, startling the two gunmen, while Jordan and Sergeant Bennett rushed in, giving them no time to pull out their weapons.

"Take your guns out nice and easy and toss them to your side," the sergeant said.

Jordan patted his thigh, and Dutch trotted to his side.

Jordan scooped both forty-fives from the ground. "You weren't even near the grave, but when you talk with your boss, tell him I know where the body is buried. Sergeant, I have a feeling there's evidence on Charles Nelson's body that could tie his death to the sports car, which, along with Tory's eyewitness account of the hit-and-run, should put an end to this."

* * *

When the doorbell rang on Christmas Day, Tory took the turkey out of the oven and set it out on the granite countertop. "Morgan, get the door. It's probably Kevin and his wife."

Not only had she invited the Bennetts to eat Christmas dinner with them but also Josh and his parents. When she'd returned last Friday from the Nelsons' property, Alana had been waiting in Tory's driveway. In light of everything that had been going on, she'd been so worried where Tory was that she'd been contemplating calling the police.

Jordan reached around her to lift the lid on the roaster. He took a deep breath. "I love that smell."

His scent mingled with the aroma of the feast she'd been preparing for Christmas dinner—a sweet potato casserole, a fruit salad, some homemade rolls, and a broccoli and cheese dish. Cleared of all charges concerning the heroin in her house, she'd thrown herself into the holidays. Just a week after the incident at the Nelsons' property, Tory still thanked God every day for protecting them. She had so much to celebrate and thank the Lord for this Christmas, especially for sending Jordan to help her.

"Mom, they're here."

"I think he's hungry." She glanced over her shoulder, Jordan only inches from her.

"So am I. The scent of that turkey has been taunting me all day, through the opening of presents and playing Morgan's new video game. I'm past starved."

She patted his cheek. "Poor, baby. Go greet our guests then come back to help me bring the food into the dining room."

"Only if you'll kiss me."

"Do I have to?" she asked in a serious tone. Then she burst out laughing. Turning, she put her arms around Jordan. "I love you. I never thought I would love again, but you have swept into my life."

"I love you, Tory. You have showed me there is too much to live for to waste away. That's all I'd done since leaving the Navy—until I met you."

Tory drew his head down and gave him a long kiss that held all her feelings for him. "More later under the mistletoe I hung up."

Someone coughed behind Tory. She looked back at Kevin in the doorway. "Dinner is almost ready."

Kevin moved into the kitchen. "I didn't want to tell you where everyone could hear. I know you want to put the incident with Charles Nelson behind you, but the DA is charging Peter London for reckless driving, leaving the scene of an accident, and vehicular manslaughter."

"So the car's paint chips on Charles's body were enough to go forward on the case?" Tory asked.

"That and your testimony. Also one of the men at the Nelson's place decided yesterday to testify that he saw Peter leaving the back entrance of the property in his sports car shortly before the accident.

Of course, that was after I told him I found his fingerprints on the knife Jordan took from your attacker. We didn't have them on record until I arrested those fellows last Friday."

"He cut a deal with the DA?" Jordan put his arm around Tory and pressed her against him.

"Yes, but he'll still serve some time. Officer Ward hasn't said anything yet. He's been suspended from the police force pending an investigation of evidence tampering. The state police will be looking into the police department and Chief Hoffman for any shady connection with Harold London. I'd have called you yesterday, but I know you all were in Denver visiting. I figure you needed the time away from here and the case after last week."

"And I used to think you didn't see the whole picture." Tory smiled and gave the sergeant a big hug. "I'm so glad you and your wife have come for Christmas dinner."

After Tory stepped back, Jordan shook the police sergeant's hand. "Do you think the police chief is involved in corruption?"

"No. He was furious when I went to him about Ward. I've worked with the man a long time, and he felt responsible for one of his officers taking a bribe. He's cooperating with the state police. I think Harold was solely behind covering up what his son did through the men he employed and Ward." Kevin turned to her. "Tory, I think Harold London just wanted you to go away or be proved unreliable. He put pressure on some important people to make your life difficult. Oh, and I almost forgot. The mechanic reported that the brakes on Nelson's new car had been tampered with. They'll be investigating the murder looking at Harold London as the prime suspect."

"Where did Bart get the money for that car?"

"Seems everything was done in cash, but what evidence there is points to the Nelsons blackmailing Harold London, using the father's dead body as leverage. We are pursuing that line of investigation to help support the murder charge against Harold."

"It sounds like Harold didn't like the

idea of being blackmailed." Jordan clasped Tory's hand.

"Right before Jordan, Morgan, and I left for Denver, my principal called and apologized for his behavior. He's discovered talking with the other students there was no truth in Mrs. Bates' allegations about me mistreating her son. When he confronted her, she confessed she blew everything out of context after Mrs. London spoke to her."

Kevin peered toward the stove. "It sure smells great, and Betsy is thrilled she didn't have to cook today. Can I help you?"

"Yes, let everyone know dinner is ready. Jordan and I will bring the food into the dining room."

Ten minutes later, Tory sat at one end of the table with Jordan at the other. Morgan sat next to Kevin and his wife while Josh, Alana, and her husband, Luke, were on the opposite side. She looked at the people she had grown to care about in Crystal Creek and thanked the Lord for bringing them into her life, especially Jordan. Their love was growing each day.

Dear Reader

Thank you for reading *Deadly Holiday*, the third book in the **Strong Women, Extraordinary Situations Series**. The first book in the series is *Deadly Hunt*. The second book is called *Deadly Intent*, highlighting another strong woman faced with dangerous circumstances. The fourth is *Deadly Countdown,* and the fifth, *Deadly Noel*.

Take care,
Margaret Daley

DEADLY COUNTDOWN

Book 4 in
Strong Women, Extraordinary Situations
by Margaret Daley

Allie Martin, a widow, has a secret protector who manipulates her life without anyone knowing until...

When Remy Broussard, an injured police officer, returns to Port David, Louisiana to visit before his medical leave is over, he discovers his childhood friend, Allie Martin, is being stalked. As Remy protects Allie and tries to find her stalker, they realize their feelings go beyond friendship.

When the stalker is found, they begin to explore the deeper feelings they have for each other, only to have a more sinister threat come between them. Will Allie be able to save Remy before he dies at the hand of a maniac?

Excerpt from
DEADLY COUNTDOWN
Book 4

Allie Martin stepped inside the post office in Port David, Louisiana to mail some packages for Aunt Evelina. Two other men stood at the counter behind Mattie Cottard, a good friend of Allie's aunt. As Allie approached the short line, she studied the back of the second man. He wore jean shorts and a black T-shirt. No mistaking that dark brown hair, cut in a neat, short style. Remy Broussard.

His grandfather, Tom, who lived near Allie and her aunt, had said he was coming home for a few weeks in July, but she hadn't known he'd arrived. It must have been last night because he would have called her right away. He'd been her best friend—her confidant—growing up.

Mattie left the counter, and the line moved up.

Allie tapped Remy's shoulder.

He glanced back, and his silver-gray gaze connected with hers.

Crinkles at the corners of his eyes deepened as he smiled and turned toward her. "I didn't expect to see you until you got off work."

Allie threw her arms around him and gave him a big hug. She'd missed him since seeing him for Mardi Gras before his motorcycle accident. "Your grandfather didn't tell me the exact time you were coming. He just said in a few days."

"You know Papere. He functions on a different timetable. I didn't tell him until I left Dallas. I wasn't sure if the doctor was going to okay the long drive."

"How are you doing since the accident?" Back in March, the news from Remy's grandfather had shaken Allie. Remy was a motorcycle police officer, and in a chase pursuing a suspect in an armed robbery, he'd crashed.

"Still on medical leave with the Dallas Police Department until the first of August. I'm so ready to get back to work."

Even as a child, Remy had hated inactivity, but then so had she. "The important thing is you're alive. Are you going to switch to driving a patrol car?" Remy had driven a motorcycle when they were younger, something she'd never liked. He loved to live dangerously, whereas she was cautious—maybe too much at times.

"I don't have plans to."

A fisherman who worked on *David's Folly*, a boat docked at the Sundowner Marina and Condos where she worked, left the counter. With a nod, Bo Fayard smiled but kept walking toward the exit.

"We'll have to get together soon," Remy said as he rotated toward Port David's postmaster and requested a roll of stamps. He paid then stepped to the side.

"I'd say tonight, but the Sundowner Marina is having a fais do-do. You know Friday nights in the summer around here. Lots of good food, Cajun music, and dancing. I hope you'll come tomorrow evening for dinner, and of course, your grandfather is welcome too." Allie slid her aunt's packages across the counter.

"Sounds good. I brought Papere into town for some supplies. See you."

As Remy walked toward the door, he limped slightly. While Remy was on the critical list at the Dallas hospital, his grandfather had left Port David, a most unusual occurrence, to be with Remy. Allie would have gone too, if he or his grandfather had said anything to her about the accident. By the time she found out, Remy had left the hospital and was at a rehab center. Remy had insisted he was on the mend and would see her when he came home.

After taking care of the postage, Allie headed outside to a brisk breeze from the Gulf. She looked up at the dark, menacing clouds blowing in. The word *ominous* flitted through her mind. Although July was hurricane season on the coast, she hadn't heard of any in the Gulf of Mexico. Hadn't the weatherman said it was going to be beautiful today? If it was going to rain, she wanted to be at work before it came. She made her way to her four-wheel drive parked in front of the Pelican General Store next door.

She opened her Jeep door and settled behind the steering wheel. A boom shook her car. Stunned, Allie froze, her heart pounding and her ears ringing.

DEADLY HUNT

Book 1 in
Strong Women, Extraordinary Situations
by Margaret Daley

All bodyguard Tess Miller wants is a vacation. But when a wounded stranger stumbles into her isolated cabin in the Arizona mountains, Tess becomes his lifeline. When Shane Burkhart opens his eyes, all he can focus on is his guardian angel leaning over him. And in the days to come he will need a guardian angel while being hunted by someone who wants him dead.

DEADLY INTENT

Book 2 in
Strong Women, Extraordinary Situations
by Margaret Daley

Texas Ranger Sarah Osborn thought she would never see her high school sweetheart, Ian O'Leary, again. But fifteen years later, Ian, an ex-FBI agent, has someone targeting him, and she's assigned to the case. Can Sarah protect Ian and her heart?

DEADLY NOEL

Book 5 in
Strong Women, Extraordinary Situations
by Margaret Daley

District attorney, Kira Davis, convicted the wrong man—Gabriel Michaels, a single dad with a young daughter. When new evidence was brought forth, his conviction was overturned, and Gabriel returned home to his ranch to put his life back together. Although Gabriel is free, the murderer of his wife is still out there and resumes killing women. In a desperate alliance, Kira and Gabriel join forces to find the true identity of the person terrorizing their town. Will they be able to forgive the past and find the killer before it's too late?

About the Author

Bestselling author, Margaret Daley, is multi-published with over 90 titles and 5 million books sold worldwide. She had written for Harlequin, Abingdon, Kensington, Dell, and Simon and Schuster. She has won multiple awards, including the prestigious Carol Award, Holt Medallion and Inspirational Readers' Choice Contest.

She has been married for over forty years and has one son and four granddaughters. When she isn't traveling, she's writing love stories, often with a suspense thread and corralling her three cats that think they rule her household.

To find out more about Margaret visit her website at *http://www.margaretdaley.com*.

Made in the USA
Las Vegas, NV
28 July 2021